THE GI

The millionaire Sholto Ransome had saved Armorel's life and then taken her under his wing as her trustee. But he was hardly a knight on a white horse— in fact as time went on she realised he was a cynical, cold-hearted rake. Could she save herself from becoming too dependent on him?

STOWAWAY

Laura had spent all her life in the South Seas, until her adoptive father's death left her stranded alone on a remote atoll. The arrival of the sloop *Sea Wind* seemed an act of Providence—except that the autocratic skipper flatly refused to take her as a passenger. So in desperation Laura decided to stow away . . .

THREE WEEKS IN EDEN

Andrea was perfectly happy to accompany her brother into the Malayan jungle for a three-week trip, although James Ferguson, the doctor who was to guide the expedition, was adamant that she should stay behind. But Andrea had no intention of taking that decision lying down!

SEPARATE BEDROOMS

When her first love ended in tragedy Antonia agreed to marry the dynamic Cal Barnard. At least, she thought, the marriage would get her away from the repressive atmosphere of Spain where she had been brought up. For the time being, Cal had agreed to a marriage 'in name only'—but could she rely on him to keep his promise indefinitely?

THE RIVER ROOM

How was Marina going to cope with working with the sophisticated, wildly attractive James Sebastian? For he made no secret of the fact that he had no objection to combining business with pleasure. And Marina was afraid not so much of him as of herself . . .

THE GIRL FROM THE SEA

BY
ANNE WEALE

MILLS & BOON LIMITED
17–19 FOLEY STREET
LONDON W1A 1DR

First published 1979
Australian copyright 1980
Philippine copyright 1980
This edition 1980

© Anne Weale 1979

ISBN 0 263 73189 8

Set in Linotype Times 10 on 11 pt.

Made and printed in Great Britain by
Richard Clay (The Chaucer Press), Ltd., Bungay, Suffolk

CHAPTER ONE

SOMETIMES, hearing the murmur of voices, or feeling a touch on her pulse, she would rouse from an uneasy doze, expecting and hoping to see the unforgettable face of the man who had saved her.

She did not know how he had done it; only that when, after weeks of struggling to survive, she had at last given up, he had found her and forced her to make one last effort to live.

But the faces she saw bending over her, and the voices which spoke kindly to her, telling her not to worry because she was in hospital and, with rest, would soon feel much better, were never those of the man at whose command she had opened her deeply sunken eyes, and in whose strong arms she had felt her own life force revive.

'You're safe now. Hang on,' he had told her.

And something in his voice had reanimated the will-power which had kept her going through all the long thirst-racked days and cold sleepless nights, at first with Aunt Rose to give her courage, and then on her own, alone in an open boat on the world's largest, deepest ocean.

Presently, as she recovered, they began to ask her questions.

'What is your name, dear?' was the first one, asked by a nurse.

'Armorel ... Armorel Baird.' Her voice was still husky, but her lips were no longer as painfully cracked as they had been when he had found her, collapsed on the

ground of the uninhabited island where she had expected
to die.

'That's a strange, pretty name,' said the nurse, who
was changing the dressings on Armorel's buttocks and
legs where the interminable days of lying in the drifting
boat had rubbed ugly sores in the skin which had been
as smooth as brown satin at the outset of the voyage.

Had she been stronger, the girl might have explained
that the name was a Gaelic one, meaning 'dweller by the
sea' and borne by many generations of her mother's
feminine forebears.

Most of them had lived and died on the west coast of
Scotland. Armorel had been born in London where,
orphaned before her third birthday, she had been
adopted by the only relation who had wanted her, a
scholarly spinster great-aunt, at that time working behind
the scenes in one of the great national museums, and
spending her weekends in a cottage on the south coast
of England. However, shortly after taking charge of the
infant, Miss Newbolt had retired with an O.B.E. and a
pension and savings sufficient to realise an eccentric
whim to live in the South Seas.

Thus it was that, unlike her ancestors, Armorel had
grown up not by the grey north Atlantic but beside an
emerald lagoon, and far from any of the influences
affecting most girls of her generation.

'Where did you come from?' asked the nurse.

Armorel told her; still unaware that in the six weeks
of her ordeal the boat in which she had drifted had been
carried almost one thousand miles from the island where
she had lived to the island where he had found her.

'Who is he——? The man who found me?' she murmured.

But the nurse had finished her task, and had gone to
relay the patient's answers to someone else.

It was curious that, after yearning for the comfort of a dry, soft bed, now that she had one again she was unable to sleep for more than an hour or two at a time.

One day, about a week after her rescue, she awoke from an afternoon nap to find a tall man with dark hair and keen grey eyes standing with folded arms at the foot of the high white hospital bed.

She recognised him instantly, and pushed herself up from the pillows with a smile of surprise and pleasure. 'I hoped you would come. If you hadn't, I was going to find you, when they discharge me. No one here seems to know who it was who found me and saved me. Nurse Tuhe said one of the crew, but I felt you must be the captain or one of the officers. They did know the name of your ship, so that was all right.' She sank back, still easily tired by any exertion.

'She's a yacht, and I'm not her captain. What made you think that?' he enquired.

'I'm not sure. Something about you.'

'I'm surprised you remember me, Miss Baird. You were very ill when I found you. I've been told not to stay more than ten minutes. May I sit down?'

'Oh, yes, please do.' As he moved a light upright chair from its place by the wall to her bedside, she added, 'You don't forget the face of the person who saves your life. I think I was very nearly dead when you found me. How *did* you find me? Why did you go to that place? It seemed just a small desert island. I could have lived there, perhaps, if I'd been stronger. But I was so weak when I reached it.'

'Yes, you were suffering from a very severe degree of dehydration. But, as no doubt they've told you, the ill effects won't be permanent. After a few more days in hospital, and two or three weeks' convalescence, you'll recover your normal health and energy.'

'I hope so,' she said, somewhat doubtfully.

'You can be sure of it,' he told her.

And from that moment she was sure, because she sensed that he was a person who would never prevaricate as perhaps the doctor and the nurses had done. This was a man who would want to be told the truth at all times, and who would not lie to her.

She said, 'You know my name, but I don't know yours.'

'Ransome ... Sholto Ransome.'

He had said he was not the yacht's captain, but perhaps he had some other rank. '*Mr* Ransome?' she queried.

He nodded. 'But why not call me Sholto, and if I may I'll use your first name? Now, to come to the point of my visit, I'm here to suggest that you should spend your convalescence on board the yacht which brought you to this hospital. Before you tell me that only a fool would suggest a cruise to someone whose recent experience of the sea has been so unpleasant, let me say that the yacht is a large one on which you can have every comfort and, even more important, once on board her you'll be free from the attentions of the media boys, by whom I'm sure you have no desire to be pestered.'

'The media boys?' she echoed blankly.

'I'm sorry: for a moment I forgot that you aren't accustomed to that sort of jargon. The word media has been corrupted to mean the newspapers and the television companies which, if they knew about your misadventure, would descend on the hospital like a swarm of flies and give you no peace.'

'Would they? Why?' she asked, in astonishment.

'Your survival was a remarkable feat. You're a girl of rare courage and endurance, and the press and television would make a big thing of your ordeal. It's only because no one knew that you and your aunt were missing, and because you were brought from where we found you on a privately owned vessel that, so far, you've escaped any publicity.'

His expression changed as he lifted an eyebrow and his firm mouth took on a sardonic twist. 'And, believe me, a storm of publicity is something which any wise person avoids if they can. I doubt if your heroism can be kept out of the headlines indefinitely, but at least on *Isola* your privacy can be preserved until you're stronger and more up to being questioned and photographed.'

'Oh, I should hate that,' she said. 'Anyway, there was nothing heroic about it. I didn't volunteer for what happened. It was forced on me ... on us.' A shudder ran through her at the memory of that terrible morning when she had woken up to find herself alone in the boat.

Sholto Ransome leaned forward and enclosed both her thin hands in one of his. His hand was not large for a man of his height and breadth of shoulder, but now that hers were so emaciated—and her fingernails white instead of their former natural pink—it covered them easily.

'Will you accept my suggestion?' he asked.

'Who does the yacht belong to? Will they want me on board?'

'She belongs to me,' was his answer. 'I am what is known as the owner, and her master is Commander Watson who used to be in the Royal Navy, and who I'm sure you will like. He's a quiet man but, if you can get him to talk, an extremely interesting one. You'll be quite safe in his charge when I've gone back to Europe. *Isola* is my holiday home, but now there are matters in Paris which need my attention, so I'm flying out on Friday.'

He rose and replaced the chair. 'My time's up for today, but I'll come and see you tomorrow. Goodbye, Armorel.'

'Goodbye ... Sholto.'

She listened to the sound of his footsteps receding along the corridor outside her room. His face which, even before, she would have recognised anywhere because of its striking bone structure and exceptionally penetrating grey eyes was now imprinted in her mind in greater detail.

She wondered if, where his yacht *Isola* was concerned, her memory was misleading her. It had seemed an enormous vessel, ten times the size of the trading schooner on which she and her aunt had depended for all their supplies and which, in the normal way, had called at their island every six weeks.

It was the schooner's failure to appear at the usual time which had made Aunt Rose decide to sail to an island twenty-five miles away where there was a village and a shop where they could replenish their dwindling stores. Armorel had for long had doubts about the seaworthiness of the boat in which they had embarked for this voyage, but it gave her no satisfaction now to have been proved right and her aunt wrong.

Rose Newbolt had been neither a loving woman nor a lovable one. But as Armorel had always supposed that the only alternative to being taken under her great-aunt's wing would have been to grow up in an orphanage, which she visualised as a most dismal and restrictive institution, she had not thought herself hard done by in spite of Aunt Rose becoming more and more despotic and tetchy as the years passed. The fact was, the girl had realised, that her aunt should have been a man, and had spent all her life resenting the restrictions and injustices afflicting females of her generation.

So although theirs had not been a fond relationship, and in all their years together they had never exchanged any gestures of affection, Armorel did grieve for her relation, and had been anxiously conscious that, with

Aunt Rose gone, she had no one in the world to turn to—or rather had had no one before Sholto Ransome's as yet unexplained kindness to her.

He must be extraordinarily rich, she thought, to be the owner of a yacht which even if *Isola* were not as large as Armorel's somewhat confused impression when they had swung her, securely strapped on a stretcher, from the yacht's tender up to her deck, must be of a considerable tonnage to need an ex-Naval commander to captain her.

Isola, she knew, was the Italian word for an island which, in a sense, a ship was. But Isola was also a name; perhaps the name of Sholto's wife. If so, it seemed rather strange that it had not been Mrs Ransome rather than her husband who had come to see Armorel in hospital and to offer the hospitality of their yacht to her. Perhaps his wife had stayed in Paris, or perhaps they had quarrelled and separated.

Her thoughts turned to Sholto's warning that if the newspapers discovered what she had been through she would be pestered by reporters. He had praised her courage and endurance, not knowing how often she had felt frightened and miserable. But her aunt had never allowed her to cry or to complain as a child, and perhaps the stiff discipline of those early years had helped to stop her breaking down in the period between her aunt's death and her own rescue.

This turned her mind back to the man who, only a few minutes before, had been seated at her bedside, his obvious fitness and dynamism making her doubly conscious of her own lost vitality. But now that he had assured her she would recover, she felt less depressed than that morning when, cleaning her teeth and looking at herself in the mirror above the handbasin, the hollowness of her cheeks and the dry condition of her formerly glossy brown hair had put her in very low spirits.

Always slender, she had lost twenty pounds, which had left her feeling all bones, except for her swollen ankles. Her hazel-green eyes, always large in relation to her other features, looked now, with dark shadows beneath them, like the huge, forlorn eyes of a bush-baby.

Since the circumstances of her growing up had not been conducive to giving much thought to her appearance, it was odd that she should mind looking the way she did now.

The hospital where they had brought her was staffed by people of many different racial origins and Dr Leong, who looked in on her several times a day, was of Chinese stock. When he came to see her in the evening, he would sit down and talk for a while.

That night he found Armorel walking back and forth on the private veranda outside her room, which also had a private bathroom of, to her, unbelievable luxury.

'How are you feeling tonight, Miss Baird?' he asked, as they sat down on the cane chairs with which the veranda was furnished.

'Oh, much better, thank you,' she told him, although in fact her shins and joints still ached, and even a little exercise made her glad to sit down and rest.

'You had a visitor, I believe?'

'Yes, Mr Ransome. Have you met him?'

'I have.'

'Did he mention that he was going to invite me to stay on his yacht while I'm convalescent? Isn't it kind of him?'

'Very kind,' the doctor agreed. 'He is also the hospital's benefactor. He has offered to provide us with some very expensive equipment for which we should otherwise have to wait a long time.'

'Has he? That's generous, isn't it? From what I've read even rich people are not always generous with their wealth. He must be a very nice man to want to look after me, and to buy equipment for the hospital.'

Instead of concurring, the doctor looked thoughtfully at the toes of his shoes before saying, 'No man is all of a piece, Miss Baird. The saint has something of the sinner in him, and vice versa. From what you have told me about yourself, your life so far has been spent in an unusual degree of isolation from your fellow human beings. Now that you are about to become more closely involved with other people, it might be wise to remember that.'

'Are you speaking about Mr Ransome?'

'No, no, of people in general. My acquaintance with Mr Ransome is of too short a duration for me to form any judgment of his character except that, as you say, he is generous with his wealth. But of course he is reputed to be a millionaire, and what would seem a fortune to you and me is of less consequence to him.'

He began to ask her one or two medical questions, after which he said goodnight, leaving her to ponder what, in spite of his denial, she felt sure had been an oblique warning not to take Sholto Ransome at face value. But why she should be on her guard with a man who had saved her life, and was now showing concern for her future welfare, Armorel could not imagine.

All the next day she looked forward to his promised visit. But when, rather earlier than the time he had come to see her the day before, she heard footsteps approaching along the corridor, they were not those for which she had been listening, but made the light clickety-click of feminine feet in high heels. The nurses wore low-heeled shoes with white canvas uppers and soles which squeaked on the polished floors, so it could not be one of them.

When, a few moments later, a lovely girl with blonde hair and arms full of parcels appeared in the doorway, Armorel could not help goggling. Very occasionally, an out-of-date copy of an American magazine had come her way, and in them she had seen photographs of girls with painted eyes and lips, wearing dramatic clothes and jewels. But never before had she seen such a girl in the flesh.

'Hello: how are you? I'm Rosalind. Sholto asked me to buy various things for you. I hope you'll like them,' the girl said, tumbling her packages on to the end of the bed and starting to undo the wrappings. 'These are a couple of nighties to wear instead of that hospital thing' —with a critical glance at the garment Armorel was wearing.

Armorel was accustomed to sleeping with no other covering than a sheet, and had found the hospital-issue nightgown an uncomfortable one which tangled round her during the night. But the nightdresses bought for her by Rosalind were made of some fabric as sheer as the wings of an insect, and coloured like clouds at sunset, one rose and the other apricot. Her thin hands flew out to touch the delicate fabric, and her eyes feasted on the colours.

'Oh... how beautiful!' she exclaimed.

'Well, they're not exactly Janet Reger. But they're not too bad. I hope they fit,' said the other girl. 'Sholto said that as far as he could tell you were about my height but thinner.'

As she unwrapped the rest of the parcels, she passed them to Armorel. 'A shower-cap ... bath essence ... talc. A bottle of hand and body lotion. Sholto said you wouldn't need make-up, but I bought some shampoo and conditioner. Can one wash one's hair in salt water, without any soap? How did you manage?'

'I didn't wash it,' said Armorel. 'It was wet a good deal of the time, from spray or when there were showers.'

'Heavens! No hairdos for six weeks. What a mess I should look!' exclaimed Rosalind.

She glanced at the other girl's hair, her expression confirming what Armorel already knew, that her hair did indeed look a mess, the more so in contrast to Rosalind's silver-gilt curls which might not be natural but formed an attractive frame for her lightly tanned face and deep blue eyes, the lids subtly shaded with colour, the lashes very thick and dark.

She was dressed in pale blue, with sandals to match tied by thin leather thongs round her ankles; and her toes were lacquered to match her fingernails. As she perched on the end of the bed, Armorel asked her, 'Are you Mrs Ransome?'

'Sholto's wife?' Rosalind looked amused. 'No, we're just good friends, as they say. I shouldn't think he'll ever marry—or not for a long time anyway.'

She produced a pack of cigarettes and offered it to Armorel who said, 'No, thank you. It was very kind of you to bring me all these things.'

'Not a bit. I love shopping.' Rosalind put a cigarette between her full, perfect lips and lit it with a slim gold lighter. She inhaled deeply and exhaled. 'Preferably in New York or Monte Carlo, but the shops here are not as hopeless as one might expect. These nighties are really quite pretty. Don't you want to put one on?'

'Yes, I will.' Armorel slid out of bed. 'Excuse me for a moment.'

It was not modesty but the wish to conceal her painful thinness from the other girl which made her disappear into the bathroom to change from the shapeless white cotton into the lace-trimmed folds of the apricot night-dress.

When she reappeared, Rosalind was scattering the wrappings all over the floor. 'There should be some slippers—— Ah, yes, here they are. They're mules, so even if they're not exactly your size you should be able to wear them.' Removing the lid from a rectangular box, she brandished a pair of gold kid mules.

From as far back as she could remember, Armorel had gone barefoot or worn cheap plimsolls. Holding on to the bedside locker, she stepped carefully into the slippers and gingerly took a few steps on the high wedge heels.

'You must take the same size as I do, an English five,' commented Rosalind. 'Oh——!'

Her ejaculation was a word which was new to Armorel, although she could read French and German as easily as English, and had a basic command of several other languages.

However, taken in conjunction with Rosalind's grimace, it was clearly an exclamation of dismay and, having said it, the other girl jumped off the bed and shot outside by the door opening on to the veranda. She returned without her cigarette, and made rapid fanning motions to dissipate the smoke in the bedroom.

At the same time Armorel heard the light stride for which she had been listening earlier and, conscious that the apricot nightgown was too revealing to be worn in front of a man, scrambled back into bed and pulled the sheet up to her armpits, so that only her now-prominent collarbones and the lacy shoulder-straps were left on view.

'Good afternoon,' Sholto said to her, as he came through the door, the top of his tall dark head clearing the lintel by a margin which confirmed that his height must be inches over six feet.

'Good afternoon,' she said, smiling.

He noticed the wrappings scattered all over the floor, and stooped to gather them up.

'You would never win a prize for tidiness, Ros.'

'I would have picked them up presently,' she replied, with a shrug, resuming her perch on the bed.

Having crunched the various pieces of wrapping and tissue paper into a compact mass, Sholto stuffed this into the shoe box which he dropped in the waste paper bin.

'Do you smoke, Armorel?' he asked, as he placed a chair by the bed.

She had lived, as Dr Leong had said, in unusual isolation, but it had not made her slow on the uptake, and his question explained Rosalind's nervous exclamation and hurried disposal of the cigarette.

When she didn't reply, not wishing to incriminate the other girl, he said, 'No, I thought not,' and levelled a sardonic glance at Rosalind.

She flushed with vexation and said petulantly, 'Oh, for God's sake, Sholto, surely I can have the occasional ciggy when you're not around. I didn't think you'd be here yet. Anyway, you used to smoke yourself, so I can't see why you're so damned pi about it.'

'But I don't now, and nor does anyone else if they have any sense. You had better sit here. I believe it's not done to sit on hospital beds.'

She took the chair, looking sulky. He fetched another for himself.

Embarrassed, and not altogether clear as to the nature of their relationship, since his manner towards Rosalind seemed more like that of a critical elder brother than a man with his beautiful mistress, Armorel said, 'It's most kind of you both to provide me with all these nice things. It puts me even more in your debt.'

'On the contrary, we're delighted to be able to help you. You'll need some other clothes shortly. When your doctor pronounces you well enough for an hour's shopping, Ros will take you to choose some day clothes. In spite of her addiction to nicotine, and her barbarous adjectives, she has very good taste in dress.'

As he said this, his cool grey eyes swept from Rosalind's long shapely legs to the curves of her opulent figure and up to her pouting red mouth. Then he smiled at her and, even as an onlooker, Armorel felt the powerful current of charm which was suddenly emanating from him. Rosalind, on the receiving end, was instantly and visibly mollified. In the space of a second her pique had changed to a smiling response to his admiring appraisal of her lovely figure.

'What a beast you are, darling,' she told him.

'Yes, but I have my redeeming features, haven't I?' was his dry reply, before he turned back to Armorel and said, 'As you know I'm leaving for Europe tomorrow, but Ros will delay her departure until you're settled on *Isola.*'

'Oh, but isn't that very inconvenient?' she asked, looking at the older girl.

'No, I don't mind,' answered Rosalind. 'Paris isn't fun at the moment, and Sholto will be tied up with board meetings. I'm quite happy to have some more time here to work up my tan.'

'By the way, this was retrieved from your boat,' said Sholto, taking from the pocket of his shirt a small plastic-wrapped package.

Armorel recognised it as the container of the note left for her by her aunt, and the letter which she herself had written to explain what had happened in case she did not survive.

'I opened the packet, and read what you'd written,' he went on. 'You were in no state to answer questions, and I thought the contents might throw some useful light on

how you had come to be in that condition, and who else
—if anyone—was involved.'

'So you know about my aunt?'

'Yes, and I've been in touch with the Resident Com-
missioner of your group of islands to tell him what happened, and to ensure that any possessions you left
behind you are held in safe keeping until you're fit to
decide whether you wish to go back, or to start a new life
elsewhere.'

'I—I know I don't want to go back. But where else
could I go?' she said helplessly.

'You're young and you'll soon be well again, and you
have exceptional qualities. The world is your oyster,' he
told her. 'But put all that out of your mind, and concentrate on getting better. In three weeks or a month I'll
come back, and we can discuss your future then.'

'Why are you being so kind to me?'

The question had been in her mind ever since the night
before.

'Because I admire courage more than any other
quality,' he said. 'And because you need help, and I can
give it. Isn't that reason enough?' He rose. 'We must go.
Au revoir, Armorel.'

'Au revoir. Goodbye, Rosalind, and thank you for doing all this shopping for me.'

As they walked away down the corridor, she heard the
other girl say, 'Poor little wretch, she's as scrawny as a
half-starved cat. Was the old aunt mad, do you suppose?'

Sholto's reply was inaudible, and Armorel guessed it
was a low-voiced admonition to Rosalind to keep her
voice down until they were safely out of earshot.

Five days later she climbed the gangway ladder of the
yacht *Isola*, which was every bit as large as she had
imagined, and, stepping on deck, was received by a thick-

set man with a neat grey beard who introduced himself as *Isola*'s master, and bade Armorel welcome.

Standing behind him was a middle-aged woman, in uniform, whom he introduced as Mrs Powers, her stewardess.

'I'll show you your stateroom, miss, shall I?' the woman said kindly. 'It's tiring, the first day out of hospital. You'll be glad of a rest before lunch.'

To Armorel, who had lived all her life in a thatched hut, the hospital had seemed luxurious. The stateroom to which she was taken was three times as large as her hospital room, with a curly white fitted carpet, and a bed draped with pale turquoise chintz matched by the cushions on the two white wicker chairs, one of which had a stool which made it into a chaise-longue.

On this Mrs Powers made her lie, with a soft white afghan tucked round her, for the stateroom was cool, being air-conditioned.

'Now you just lie quiet for half an hour, and you'll feel refreshed when I come to call you for lunch,' the stewardess advised her. 'Mr Ransome left strict instructions that we shouldn't allow you to overdo things. She's a strong-minded young lady, Mrs Powers. You must keep her in order, he told me. So you mustn't go getting me into trouble by not being as well as you should be when he comes back, miss.'

Am I strong-minded? Armorel wondered, when the stewardess had left her on her own. *He* is strong-minded, that's certain. A man who wants his own way, and gets it, I should imagine.

Her gaze roved around her quarters which included, through a mirrored door, a rose-coloured marble bathroom with a shower, pink towels on hot rails, scales to check her increase in weight, a dryer for her hair, and cupboards full of creams and lotions.

The stateroom itself was equally fully equipped. Beside the bed was a telephone which, as Mrs Powers had explained, had press-buttons for calling the duty stewardess and steward, the galley, the bridge and the signals room.

Books in shiny new dust-jackets filled a tall bank of shelves, with a sloping rack for magazines, and a smaller glass-enclosed shelf for what, so Mrs Powers told her, were cassettes for the built-in music deck. Besides these, there were flowers and paintings, and delicate porcelain ornaments beyond Armorel's most fanciful day-dreams.

At the time of her admission to hospital, tests had shown her to be anaemic, and of this she was still not cured, although her haemoglobin level had improved. Another result of being cast away for so long was that, although Dr Leong had warned her against over-eating, and the hospital meals had been adequate for her body's needs, she was always hungry. The visions of food which had obsessed her during her ordeal still played a large part in her thoughts.

To her relief, she had lunch alone with Rosalind, and afterwards while she lay on a lounger under the awning, the other girl lay in the full sun, on a towel spread over an air-bed. She was wearing a minimal bikini, and was lavishly anointed with coconut butter. Her silver-gilt hair she kept covered, explaining that it was bleached, and sunlight was death to bleached hair.

'Have you known Sholto long?' Armorel asked, watching the yacht's wake spreading as she cruised on a calm blue sea with only a light breeze to flutter the fringe of the awning.

Rosalind yawned. 'About four months. He's quite a dish, don't you think?'

'I'm not sure what a dish is.'

The older girl laughed. 'Talking to you is like talking to someone from Mars! One has to explain so many

things. A dish is a man who switches you on ... lights
your fire ... makes you want to go to bed with him.
Have you never felt like that about a man?'

Armorel shook her head. 'But I haven't met many.'

'No, I suppose not. How old are you?'

'Almost nineteen.'

'My God! I couldn't count all the men I'd known by
the time I was nineteen.' Rosalind rolled on her stomach
and reached for a cigarette. Since Sholto's departure,
Armorel had seldom seen her without one between her
long fingers.

'How old are you?' she enquired.

'Twenty-three.'

'And Sholto?'

'D'you know, I've never asked him. Thirty years
younger than most of the men with his assets, that's for
sure. Most millionaires are so dreary that I couldn't
bear it, but Sholto's terrific—in bed, I mean. Am I
shocking you?' She took off her large tinted glasses the
better to see Armorel's expression. 'Did your eccentric
old aunt bring you up by the rules of her day when nice
girls were always virgins until they got married?'

'Aunt Rose disapproved of marriage. She said there
were better things to do with one's life than to wait on a
man.'

'Hear, hear!' murmured Rosalind. 'If you must get
married, look for a man who's rich enough to pay other
people to wait on him. But in that case, alas, usually he
doesn't want a wife, or even a permanent girl-friend. He
prefers a new model every so often. As Sholto will soon,
I suppose. But meanwhile I'm having a great time. He
switches me on. He buys me whatever I want, and takes
me to fabulous places. Live for today is my motto.'

With which statement she crushed out the half-smoked
cigarette, and turned on her back and announced that
she was going to sleep.

Armorel remained awake, thinking over Rosalind's maxim, and arriving at the conclusion that, for her, it was as unacceptable as her aunt's idea of how to live. Both their outlooks excluded love which, from what she had read in the dozens of mildew-stained volumes which her aunt had shipped out from England, was the summit of human experience.

Presently, seeing that Rosalind had fallen into a deep sleep from which she was unlikely to wake for some time, Armorel quietly got up and went for a walk along the deck leading forward. Each day her legs grew stronger, but it would be a long time, she felt, before she could run and swim as she had on her home island.

One or two of the nurses in the hospital, learning that she was to convalesce on *Isola*, had expressed astonishment that she should be prepared to go back to sea so soon, if indeed ever.

But, pausing to lean on the port rails and rest a few minutes, Armorel looked down at the element with which, although it had always been part of her life, she was now so intimately acquainted, and felt no fear of the dark cobalt depths below her.

Hearing a slight sound behind her, she turned to see a fair-haired young man of about her own age passing along the deck behind her. He was dressed in the same sort of uniform as the Chief Steward, Mr Bates, who had served their lunch. As she looked at him, he checked his pace and said politely, 'Good afternoon, miss. Is there anything I can get for you?'

She hesitated, not wishing to be a nuisance. But her thirst was as persistent as her hunger, and after a moment she said, 'Do you think I could have another bottle of that delicious iced water I had with my lunch?'

'Certainly, miss. I'll fetch it for you immediately. Are you on your way to the forward deck? You'll find some comfortable chairs there.'

'Shall I? Thank you.'

She continued along the deck, her hair, now a good deal improved by several applications of the conditioner bought for her by Ros, blown back from her face by the stronger breeze coming over the bows.

It was not long before the young steward reappeared with a tray on which, standing in a bucket of crushed ice, was another bottle of the French spring water she had drunk with her lunch in preference to the white wine which Ros had asked for.

The steward set the tray on the table beside her chair and, having uncapped the bottle, poured some of the slightly effervescent water into a long-stemmed glass. Then, as Mr Bates had, he replaced the original cap with one of a different type which kept the water from going flat but which could be removed with the fingers.

'Thank you very much. I've never tasted such good water, and it's still a luxury to me to be able to drink as much as I want,' she said.

'Yes, I imagine it must be. Can I get you something to read, miss? Some fashion magazines perhaps?'

'It's kind of you, but I shall be quite happy just sitting here. Have you been on *Isola* for long?'

'Not very long.' His pleasant blue-grey eyes flicked a glance at something behind and above her. 'Will you excuse me, miss?'

When he had left her, Armorel sipped the glass of water. She did not have to look round to guess that his glance had been directed at the yacht's bridge, and she wondered why he should seem to be nervous of being seen in conversation with her. Both Mrs Powers and Mr Bates had chatted freely to her, but perhaps the more junior members of the crew were discouraged from talking to the passengers.

The young steward puzzled her slightly, for although

they had exchanged only a few words, she had noticed that he spoke with the same accent as Sholto rather than with Mr Bates' type of voice and—because her ideas of life in Europe were based on her great aunt's attitudes—she thought he seemed more like one of the yacht's junior officers than a junior steward.

That evening, before dinner, the four other officers were presented to her. She had felt shy of meeting them, but they soon put her at her ease. The circumstances which had brought her among them were not mentioned, and the talk at the dinner table was mainly of books. They all seemed to read a great deal, and as Armorel was widely read in the classics of European literature if not in contemporary or lighter fields, she had no difficulty in taking her share of the conversation. It was Ros who was rather left out as, by her own admission, she never read anything but *Vogue, Harpers & Queen* and the leading American magazines for women.

However, she looked very glamorous in a low-cut short summer evening dress of azure chiffon and, on Mrs Powers' advice, Armorel had changed into a pretty cotton voile dress. But hers had been chosen to hide her shoulders and arms until they had recovered their normal contours, and she was less self-conscious about them.

Armorel went to bed early and by the next morning—for she still had difficulty in sleeping for long at a time—had devoured a recently-published novel chosen from those in her stateroom. It opened her eyes to the fact that life in her native land had changed a great deal since she and Miss Newbolt had left it, sixteen years ago, and had changed even more since her great-aunt's formative years, before and after the First World War.

As she ate her breakfast, brought to her in bed by Mrs Powers, she marvelled at the luxury of her present life compared with the privations of a month ago.

During the morning she discovered that the yacht's amenities included a beauty treatment room where two more women of about the same age as Mrs Powers ensured that when Sholto had a party of guests on board, the women's hair and nails remained as perfectly coiffed and manicured as in their normal habitat.

While Ros was being given a massage by Mrs Dunne, Miss Shotley attended to Armorel's nails.

'They're a nice shape, but very neglected, Miss Baird. They weren't always this pale colour, were they?'

'No, they used to be pink.'

'And will be again in a few months. Look, where I've pushed back the cuticle, you can already see the regrowth.'

Three days later *Isola* berthed at an island with an airstrip an hour's flight from an international airport from which Ros could fly to Paris to rejoin Sholto.

Armorel was not altogether sorry to see her go. Accustomed as she was, even before being a castaway, to hours of solitude and silence, the older girl's idle chatter had begun to weary her a little.

As the days passed she began to sleep better, her aches diminished, and her reflection in the mirror bore less resemblance to a bush-baby and more to her former healthy self.

Every day she saw the young steward, and twice she heard him addressed by his surname, Harper. But the first time she had any proper conversation with him was the day the yacht anchored off an island with an easily navigable reef where most of the crew went ashore to swim in the lagoon, and to have a barbecue lunch on the beach.

Although she had bathed in the small pool aboard the yacht, Armorel had not swum as she was accustomed to swimming since the last day before her ill-fated voyage

with her great-aunt. While the barbecue was being prepared under the direction of Mr Bates, she slipped away
from the others to test the extent of her recovery by
seeing how far she could swim without tiring.

The green and white bikini which she had on under her
sun-dress was one left aboard *Isola* by a careless guest,
and put aside by Mrs Powers. It was as brief as it could
be, but even so Armorel would have preferred to bathe
in the nude as she had been accustomed to do on the
island which was the only home she could remember.

Out of sight of the rest of the shore party, she took
off her dress and waded into the water until, at waist
depth, she plunged forward and disappeared under the
surface to come up, some distance away, with her long
hair streaming behind her.

Unaware of being under surveillance, she struck out
with a fast crawl and swam until her arms ached with the
unaccustomed exertion. Then, satisfied that it would not
be too much longer before she was fully recovered, she
turned for the shore and stumbled dizzily out of the water
to collapse on the sand and lie gazing up at the sky, pant-
ing and fatigued but pleased with the result of her test.

'Are you all right, Miss Baird?'

The quiet, concerned voice made her struggle into a
sitting position. Steward Harper, wearing bathing trunks
instead of his usual spruce uniform, was standing a few
yards away.

'Oh, hello,' she said, smiling at him. 'Yes ... yes, I'm
fine. A bit breathless, but I suppose that's only to be
expected.'

'You're a fantastic swimmer,' he said. 'You cut through
the water like a shark.'

'I've swum almost every day of my life. Do you like
the water?'

'Who wouldn't—here?' he replied, with a glance at the

translucent shallows which shaded from aquamarine to emerald in the deeper water.

'Now I'm covered with sand. I shall have to go in and rinse off. Are you coming in?' she enquired, since he did not seem to have bathed yet.

She thought he hesitated before assenting. They ran in together and both took a splashy header which he followed with a fast crawl for perhaps twenty yards while Armorel followed more leisurely.

'I don't know your name,' she said, when they were both treading water not far from each other.

'Harper.'

'I meant your first name.'

'Kit.'

'Mine's Armorel, as you probably know. You don't have to call me Miss Baird today, do you?'

'I think I probably should.'

'Why? I've got the impression from the books I've been reading about England that life is completely different from the way it was in my aunt's time ... that today everybody is equal, at least in their off-duty hours.'

'I suppose they are—up to a point. But I'm in a special position.'

'Are you? Why?' she enquired.

This time there was no doubt about his hesitation, but eventually he said, 'I'm not really a steward. It's a temporary job in my case, but I'm more or less on my honour to do the thing properly, as if it were permanent.'

'If you're not really a steward, what are you?'

'Nothing, as yet. I only left school a few months ago. When I've finished my stint as a steward, I'm going to start reading law. It's a caprice of my father's that all his children, between a privileged childhood and a probably privileged adult life should have a taste of being in a menial position. My father started with nothing and he has a bit of a phobia about people who squander their money, or who take the good life for granted. So my eldest sister had to do a six-month stint behind a counter in one of the big stores in London which, being an outdoor type, she really loathed. But Dad said if she hadn't the grit to stick for six months what thousands of people have to stick for a lifetime, he wasn't going to help her to set up a riding stable.'

As he talked they had been swimming back towards the beach. Now, with her feet on sand and her torso clear of the water, Armorel twisted her hair into one thick skein and wrung it out.

'Do you loathe being a steward?' she asked.

'Oh, no, mine's a cushy number compared with Deb's. My mother set this up for me. Mr Ransome's sister is a friend of hers, and Ma has this dotty idea that I'm delicate because I missed a couple of terms at school after being in a car smash.'

'You certainly don't look delicate,' she said, with a sideways glance.

Kit Harper was lightly built, but well-knit.

'No, I'm not. I'm as tough as the next guy. But it will take years to convince my mother that I'm not in danger of disintegrating. So, not altogether with Dad's approval, she arranged this what you might call working cruise for me. But my father wouldn't be pleased if he thought I was fraternising with the passengers ... Miss Baird,' he added, with a grin.

'Mr Bates talks to me a lot. I know his life history,' she said. 'I'm sure there can be no objection to your talking to me today when everyone is fraternising, even Commander Watson.'

'Except that it will make it harder to keep a respectful distance tomorrow.' As she had glanced at his figure a few moments earlier, now he looked at hers. 'Mr Ransome won't recognise you when he comes back. I was on duty at the picnic the day he found you, and even a small, puny man could have carried you then.'

'I wish you would tell me what happened. I asked Rosalind, but she wasn't there, apparently.'

'No, Miss Plummer wasn't on board that day. As she may have told you, she'd lost a filling in a tooth leaving the nerve exposed. It was so painful that Mr Ransome arranged to have her picked up by helicopter and taken to the nearest dentist. The picnic was for the six guests we had with us then, but I think Mr Ransome had had enough of their company as, after lunch, he went off by himself. He doesn't suffer fools gladly and one of the women was a total bird-brain, and always gushing away at him. When he came back with you in his arms everyone thought you were too far gone to recover. But look at you now! A stunner, if I may say so . . . miss.'

She laughed and coloured a little. The scales and her mirror told her that she had recovered most of the lost weight and with it the curves she had had before her ordeal, but no young man had ever told her that she was a stunner and, although she knew he was exaggerating, it was a nice thing to hear.

'What puzzles me is how Mr Ransome managed to keep the story out of the press,' Kit went on. 'It was easy enough to make the crew keep their mouths shut. We were all threatened with the sack if we breathed a word. But I don't know how he managed to gag that fool of a woman, except maybe by putting pressure on her husband. Mr Ransome is a pretty ruthless character, they say, and *his* phobia is publicity.' His attractive grin reappeared. 'Which is why his sister and my mother don't know too much about how he carries on in his private life.'

'What do you mean?' asked Armorel.

Suddenly Kit looked uncomfortable. 'Oh, nothing really. I expect half the tales are ship's gossip, and very much exaggerated.'

'What are the tales?'

'His nickname is Randy Ransome.' He saw that this meant nothing to her, and explained, 'It means he's a terrific womaniser. You realised that he and Miss Plummer were——' He left the remark unfinished. 'Let's change the subject. I should never have brought it up. I'm working for him, and I like him.'

'I owe him my life,' she said simply.

'Yes, it was damned lucky for you that the woman did bore him into going off alone,' he agreed.

They had been strolling back towards the barbecue party, and were now within earshot of the others. As they joined them, Armorel became aware that most of the men were eyeing her in a way which made her wish she was not quite so scantily clad.

She was used to being next to naked, but unused to people looking at her, and while she had not minded Kit's appraisal, it was a different matter to have a whole group of men looking at her breasts, her navel and the bows of white cord which secured the bottom of the bikini. They did not continue to leer at her, as one of the crew of the supply schooner had once done, but although they soon looked away, their concerted scrutiny made a deep blush suffuse her face. Hurriedly slipping on her sun-dress, she went to join the three women members of the crew.

A few days later she heard Mrs Powers and Mrs Dunne discussing her, and what she overheard them say before she realised that she was eavesdropping and should not continue to listen to a conversation not meant for her ears, left her troubled and uneasy.

'Oh, yes, she's a beauty all right. Not that you'd ever

have guessed it when they brought her on board more dead than alive,' said Mrs Powers. 'If you want my opinion, this little girl knocks spots off that Rosalind Plummer. Not that we're likely to see *her* again, I fancy. She's had her run, if you ask me. There'll be a new one in tow before long.'

Mrs Dunne volunteered her views. 'I agree with you, Muriel. You can't compare young Miss Baird with the Plummer girl. This one's as innocent as a baby. You could tell that by the way she coloured up when all the men's eyes nearly popped out on stalks when they saw how she looked in a bathing suit. There was nothing innocent about the other one. She knew all the answers long before His Nibs laid a finger on her.'

'Well, all I hope, Ida my dear, is that when Mr Ransome finds out what a gorgeous young thing this one is, he won't take it into his head to make her the next on the list. In the normal way I won't hear a word said against him, not since he was so good to Eddy, paying for a private room in the Royal Marsden Hospital and everything. But I have to admit Mr R. is a terror with women. Not that most men wouldn't be the same if they had his opportunities, I daresay.'

It was at this juncture that Armorel realised she must not listen to any more. Deeply disturbed by the little she had heard, she went to her stateroom and stared at herself in the mirror. Was she really a beauty? And was it possible that the man she thought of as her benefactor might turn out to be an unscrupulous lecher who would expect her to repay his generosity by sharing his bed?

Two weeks had passed, and Armorel had managed to put the two women's forebodings on her behalf to the back of her mind, when Commander Watson mentioned to her that *Isola*'s owner was on his way back to the Pacific, and would be rejoining the yacht in two days' time.

'Is Miss Plummer coming with him?' she asked.

'I believe not, Miss Baird.'

It seemed to her that his gaze rested rather gravely upon her. However as his manner was habitually sombre rather than jovial, perhaps she imagined the tinge of concern in his expression.

Since the barbecue party she had had no conversation with Kit. Her lunch always was served by Mr Bates or another steward. Kit seemed to be occupied with behind-the-scenes tasks during the day, and did not appear until dinner when, although sometimes she managed to catch his eye and smile at him, his response was guarded in the extreme. Had she not known the reason for this, she would have felt snubbed by his coolness.

However the day before Sholto's return, she chanced to run into Kit in one of the between-decks corridors and, although he would have passed on after saying a formal good morning, she stopped him by catching his arm and saying, 'Can you spare five minutes? I must talk to you.'

He looked rather startled and wary but, after a second or two, said, 'We'd better go in there'—indicating a door not far from where they were standing.

It led into a store where the bulkheads were lined with shelves bearing neatly stacked boxes of tissues, huge drums of washing powder and what, at a glance, Armorel took to be all the bathroom, laundry and cleaning products required on a yacht which, in addition to her crew could, so Mr Bates had told her, accommodate twenty passengers.

'What's the trouble,' asked Kit, as he closed the door.

'No trouble . . . only a problem. Now that Mr Ransome is coming back, I've been thinking about my future. I should like to go back to England where I was born, and I wanted to ask your advice on whether I could find work there, and earn enough to support myself.'

He studied her for some moments, his expression not unlike Commander Watson's when she had asked him if Sholto would be accompanied by Rosalind.

'I'm not sure,' he said, at length. 'From your conversations with the officers at dinner, I gather you're pretty well read, but nowadays, in England, it's difficult to get a start on a worthwhile career without passing examinations and getting things called O levels and A levels. Have you ever done any maths or sciences?'

'Oh, yes,' she said, and outlined the programme of education organised for her by her aunt.

'Good lord! It sounds as if you're a darned sight better educated than I am,' was his comment. 'But the thing is to be able to prove it. I really don't think you need worry. I'm sure Mr Ransome won't expect you to fend for yourself just because you've recovered your strength. Obviously you need more help, and I'm sure he'll arrange something for you.'

'I'm sure he would,' she agreed, 'but I don't want to impose on his kindness any longer than is strictly necessary. I have to learn to fend for myself. You told me your sister had spent six months working in one of the big stores in London. Would a job like that pay enough to cover one's living expenses?'

'I doubt it. Dad didn't go as far as to make Deb live in digs. Our home isn't far outside London and she commuted, as I should think the majority of girls do. Some can afford to share flats, but it can be a tricky arrangement if the sharers have habits which jar on each other.'

'Yes, I don't think I should like that. I'd prefer a room of my own—a bed-sitter with cooking arrangements,' said Armorel.

'You could be very lonely on your own in a city like

London. It takes time to make friends.'

'I shouldn't be lonely,' she assured him. 'I've been
alone all my life except for Aunt Rose. Sometimes we
hardly spoke to each other for days. She was a very
withdrawn person. Besides, in London I should have all
those wonderful shop windows to look at, and all the
museums and art galleries to visit.'

'God! Half an hour in a museum is enough for me,'
remarked Kit. 'But I suppose if you like——' He broke
off as the door opened and Mr Bates entered, looking
surprised to find them there.

'What are you doing here, Harper?' he asked, with a
glance at Armorel which she interpreted as the same
question, unspoken, directed at her.

'Miss Baird was asking me about life in England.'

'I see. Well, you're not off duty, my lad, so get back
to work now. Look sharp!'

Armorel saw Kit's lips tighten, but whatever retort
was on the tip of his tongue he managed to suppress it.
Without a word he left the store.

'I think you'll find Commander Watson and Mr Ransome the best people to advise you, miss,' said the Chief
Steward, when they were alone.

'Possibly, but Kit has sisters of about my age. I'm
sorry I distracted him from his duties, Mr Bates. It was
entirely my fault.'

'No need to apologise, miss.'

He held the door open for her, and Armorel went on
deck to continue to ponder the problem of her future.

At the moment when, the next day, Sholto's flight was
coming in to land at the airport of the island where *Isola*
was berthed by the deep water dock, Armorel, on his
instructions, was having a thorough medical check.

When she returned to the yacht, he was on board but

not on deck. She did not see him until shortly before dinner, by which time they were at sea again.

Although among the clothes which Rosalind had helped her to choose—a far more extensive wardrobe than Armorel had thought necessary, but Rosalind had overruled her—there were two pretty short dinner dresses, she chose to put on a plain cream silk shirt and skirt.

Mrs Powers did not quarrel with this choice, nor with Armorel's decision to wear her long hair tied back instead of loose on her shoulders.

'You'd look a picture if you were dressed in a sack, miss,' she said, when Armorel was ready. 'You're like my lovely Lady Emily'—a reference to the wife of a previous employer. 'She had the gift of looking elegant even in her old gardening clothes, and you have it, too.'

'Do I?' Armorel looked at herself in the long mirror.

She knew that she had changed a great deal since Sholto had last seen her, but whether he, accustomed to beautiful women, would find her looks to his taste remained to be seen. She very much hoped not. She did not want her present warm gratitude to be soured, as it must be if he tried to involve her in the kind of relationship he had had with Rosalind. But she could see in Mrs Powers' eyes the look of someone watching a lamb go to the slaughter, and it was with deep apprehension that she went on deck to join him for dinner.

CHAPTER TWO

HE was standing by the rails, with his back to her, and his hands resting on the top rail as he looked at the sea, now sparkling silver in the Pacific moonlight.

At nightfall the white-fringed blue awning which protected the lunch-table from the full strength of the sun was wound out of sight and the table left open to the southern night sky, and lit by candles, their flames protected from breezes by glass shades.

Armorel swallowed to clear a feeling of constriction in her throat which she knew was caused only by nervousness.

'Good evening, Mr Ransome,' she said quietly.

He turned to face her and, as their eyes met, his had the detached expression of someone deeply preoccupied. Then, an instant later, she had his full attention, and his steely grey gaze swept down from her face to her feet and, more slowly, back to her face in a look which made her feel as if the silk shirt and skirt had suddenly melted away and left her standing before him in nothing but her flimsy underthings.

It gave her a disconcerting insight into the feelings of girls sold in slave markets centuries ago. She had an unpleasant sense of being at the mercy of a ruthless and highly sensual man who would use her body as he liked, and care nothing for her mind, or whether she liked or disliked him, so long as he found her pleasing.

But before she could show her resentment at being looked over like a girl on an auction block, he said, 'Good evening. I shouldn't have recognised you.' And, as he spoke, his eyes became cool and impersonal, as if the hot blaze of lust had never been in them.

'I'm glad to see you have recovered so well,' he went on. 'Did your medical check today confirm that you're as healthy as you look?'

'Yes, thank you. There's nothing wrong with me now —thanks to the wonderful convalescence I've had.'

'Good. Then we can proceed to the subject of your future,' he said briskly. 'Shall we dine?'—moving to the table and drawing out one of the chairs for her.

Before taking his own place opposite, he touched the bell which summoned the Chief Steward or one of his subordinates.

As they waited for someone to come, he said, 'Have you had any thoughts on the matter?'

'I should like to go back to England, but perhaps that wouldn't be practicable.'

'Why shouldn't it be?' he enquired.

As he took the napkin from his side plate and shook out its fine linen folds, she remembered noticing before the shapeliness of his hands, their structure clearly defined under the sun-tanned skin. They were strong hands with muscular wrists, and although it was clear that his life must exclude any manual work, equally obviously it must include a great deal of physical activity for him to be so lean and limber.

'In the note my aunt left—which you read—she mentioned some funds she had left for me, but I don't know how much there will be, or whether it would cover the fare and keep me going until I find work.'

'What work had you in mind?'

'Anything I can get.'

At this point Mr Bates appeared, and served the first course, a dish which, having had it before and asked its name, she recognised as *oeufs à la Chimay*, eggs stuffed with mushrooms and baked in a cheese sauce.

'Will you have some wine this evening, miss?' the Chief Steward asked.

'No, thank you. Just my usual water.'

'You don't care for wine?' enquired Sholto.

'I've never tried it. The water you have is so good.'

'High time you learnt to enjoy wine.' He signalled to Bates to fill her glass. 'This is a *Pouilly-Fuissé*, one of the great white Burgundies. There are people who think one should never drink wine with an egg dish, but I disagree.'

She took a small, cautious sip, liking the taste but afraid of its effect on her wits. He was not to know it, but her aunt had been a fanatical teetotaller who had frequently lectured Armorel on the evil influence of alcohol.

According to Miss Newbolt, it was owing to the fact that her niece, Armorel's mother, had been made tipsy at a party by a thoroughly unsuitable young man that Armorel owed her existence. Being the child of an elderly widower with narrow views, and being advised by her aunt that she would be compounding her error if she married the young man, Armorel's mother had decided to bring up her baby on her own. This she had managed to do until she was killed and, although Rose Newbolt had often deplored the original folly, she had given her niece credit for shouldering her responsibility.

'You should never settle for "anything",' said Sholto, reverting to Armorel's last remark before the arrival of their meal.

'Sometimes one must,' she said dryly. 'Naturally one would prefer to eat *oeufs à la Chimay* and drink *Pouilly-Fuissé*, but there are circumstances in which some raw fish and a cup of rain can seem even more delicious.'

He flashed a narrowed glance at her, and she thought she might have annoyed him. But a gleam of amusement lit his eyes, and he said, 'Very true. But your circumstances at present are not such that you need accept any form of subsistence. If your aunt's funds should prove inadequate, I shall be glad to assist you.'

She repeated what she had said to Kit. 'You're very kind, and I'm grateful beyond expression, but I must start to fend for myself.'

'Why?'

'Because ... because everyone should.'

'When they are adult—yes, certainly. You have yet to reach that estate. Alone in an alien environment, you would be as vulnerable as an infant turtle between being hatched and reaching the sea.' Before she could answer, he continued, 'You seem to have a good French accent. Do you speak French?'

'A little. But I learnt it from books and gramophone records which were made before I was born, so my French is probably old-fashioned.'

'As is your English,' he told her. 'A gramophone now is known as a record-player, or sometimes a music deck, and a record is often called a disc. But I'm sure it won't take you long to pick up the current idioms—unfortunately! I find your archaisms refreshing!'

He made this last comment in French, and she answered in the same language, 'Would speaking one or two languages enable me to get a job?'

'They would probably need to be allied to such basic skills as typing and speed-writing. However, I think you must put out of your mind any possibility of immediate independence. To change from one environment to another is never a quick business. To use another analogy, you're like a diver who, if he surfaces too quickly from deep water, will have an attack of the "bends". He has to return to his natural element slowly, as you must.'

Armorel laid down her fork. 'How can I do that?' she asked him.

'By going to a school I know of; a school for girls of your age who are finishing their education by learning how to cook, how to entertain, how to organise their future households. Those are things which all women should know, whether or not they also have careers in the outside world.'

'I've read about finishing schools, but they're for the daughters of very rich people.'

He reached out to touch the bell and recall the steward. 'I am very rich, Armorel, and although I'm not old enough to be your father, I'm happy to stand proxy for him. Who was your father?'

She hesitated. 'I don't know. I don't even know his name. Baird was my mother's surname. They weren't married, and if she had any photographs of him they must have been destroyed by my great-aunt after my mother was killed. I was only two, so I don't remember her.'

'And your mother's parents? Have you had any contact with them?'

'No. My grandmother—my great-aunt's sister—died before I was born, and my grandfather, who was much older, is unlikely to be alive now. There were some other relations but, had it not been for my aunt, I should have been put in an orphanage. So I don't feel inclined to seek them out.'

'I should think it's more likely that you would have been adopted,' he said.

The main course was brought, a simple but perfect salad accompanied by the delicious bread made daily by the French chef in charge of *Isola*'s galley.

It was only when Bates replenished her wine-glass that Armorel realised she had absentmindedly drunk nearly all he had poured out the first time. She would have to be careful not to do the same with the second glassful.

'You say you're very rich. How did you make your fortune?' she asked, when they were alone again.

'The basis was made by my grandfather who went to England from central Europe with an unpronounceable foreign name which he subsequently changed to Ransome, and no money but plenty of acumen. My father had little acumen, but he married a girl who came from an old English family and knew how to spend money wisely on things of lasting beauty and value, and not on the flashy rubbish which tends to attract the newly rich. I like to think that I've inherited both my grandfather's peasant shrewdness and my mother's cultivated taste.'

'Have you any brothers and sisters?'

'One elder sister.'

'Oh, yes, of course, the one who's——' She stopped short, remembering where and from whom she had heard of his sister. 'I—I believe Rosalind mentioned her.'

A strange and very cold expression came over his features. All the planes of his face seemed to harden, making her sharply aware of the broad, high cheekbones which he must have inherited from his Slav grandfather, and the forceful jut of the chin beneath the now compressed lips.

'Never try to mislead me, Armorel,' he said, in a pleasant tone which did not accord with the icy glitter in his eyes. 'You will not succeed, and I'm not kindly disposed to those who take me for a fool.'

'W-what do you mean?' she stammered nervously.

'You would not have heard of my sister from Rosalind—they've never met. I don't think you are so unversed in the ways of the world that you were not aware of the nature of my relationship with Rosalind. However,

I prefer to keep my personal life and my family relationships quite separate.'

She said nothing, crushed by his scorn, and annoyed with herself for having incurred his displeasure so soon after his arrival.

'Probably my sister was mentioned to you by Harper who, to use the vernacular of the young in England, has been "chatting you up", it would appear.'

'If it means that we've talked sometimes—yes.'

'It means rather more than that. It implies the hope of more than a casual acquaintance, which Harper seems to have achieved if you now find it necessary to seek the privacy of a store-room for your "talks" with each other,' was his sardonic answer.

Her discomfiture gave place to anger. 'I hadn't realised that I was under surveillance, and everything I did was reported back to you,' she said, her own small firm chin lifting indignantly. 'It was Mr Bates who misled you if he implied that anything clandestine was going on when he interrupted us talking in the store-room. I was merely asking Kit's opinion about my chances of supporting myself in England.'

Sholto lifted an eyebrow. 'The fact that you use his first name suggests a greater degree of intimacy than is usual between the stewards and my guests.'

'He isn't the same as the other stewards, although he feels duty bound to behave as if he were. *He* tries to avoid talking to me. It was I who ... who pressed him into it.'

'And was it you who suggested going into the store for your tête-à-tête?'

'No—no, that was his suggestion. But I really can't see any harm in it.'

'Perhaps there was none,' he agreed. 'But any girl as pretty as you are who goes into a secluded place with a young man like Harper shouldn't be surprised to find herself being kissed by him. Perhaps the idea appealed to you?'

'It never crossed my mind.'

'I'm sure it crossed his,' he said dryly. 'And probably much more besides. One of the first lessons you'll have to learn is that most of the men you meet will want to make love to you, and many of them will attempt it. If you want to avoid embarrassment, you'll have to learn to behave with a good deal more discretion than you showed with young Harper.'

She looked him squarely in the face. 'Must I be on my guard with you, too? Because, if I must, I'd rather you put me ashore at the nearest inhabited island.'

A gleam of humour returned to the steely grey eyes on the opposite side of the dining-table. 'No,' he said, 'as it happens I'm one of the few men whom you can be sure has no designs on you. I have a number of vices, but they don't include the seduction of young girls such as yourself.'

'Well, that's a relief,' she said frankly.

It was only when Sholto laughed that she realised so outspoken a reaction was not very diplomatic.

'I'm sorry; I didn't mean that you're ... that you aren't——' she began, in confusion.

'Oh, don't spoil it by apologising. I find your candour engaging in a world full of sycophants. If you always say what you think to me, we shall get on a great deal better than if you butter me up. Will you have some more salad?'

'No, thank you, not for me.' As she watched him helping himself, it struck her that only a man with very little personal vanity would have laughed at her unguarded statement.

When she had dined with the officers, the cheese had

always come last. But evidently Sholto preferred to end his meals in what she knew to be the French way, with the cheese coming before the pudding which, tonight, was a light and refreshing lemon sorbet.

With the coffee, he introduced her to a Balkan liqueur called slivovitz which he said was made from small blue plums, and which had a faint almond flavour from the crushed stones used in its manufacture.

After dinner, he took her below to the yacht's main saloon which Armorel had sometimes glimpsed when it was being vacuumed and dusted, but which so far she had never entered. Tonight it was lit by picture lights, and by several silk-shaded table lamps made from tall blue and white Chinese jars. The furnishings were restfully plain, the cream linen covers exactly matching the fitted carpet overlaid with three fine Persian rugs which she recognised for what they were because Miss Newbolt's possessions had included two worn and shabby ones.

Mrs Powers had told her that the pannelling in the saloon had come from an English mansion which had been demolished, and the mellow old wood, first put up in George I's reign, was the background for perhaps a dozen paintings, some hung on their own, some in groups.

In Sholto's absence, Rosalind had often switched on her transistor radio and tuned to a station playing music which, to Armorel's unaccustomed ears, had sounded painfully discordant. Often the lyrics, although sung in English, had been incomprehensible to her.

But while she was standing, looking at one of the paintings, the saloon was suddenly filled with notes which, because their clarity and tone were so infinitely superior to the scratchy reproduction of sound on Miss Newbolt's old hand-wound gramophone, for an instant she hardly recognised as the opening bars of one of her favourite piano concertos.

She sat down and closed her eyes, re-opening them after some moments to say, in delighted astonishment, 'It's like being at a real concert!'

'Rather better, in my opinion,' was Sholto's reply. 'I dislike being forced to sit still, and a background of coughing and rustling.'

To her surprise, in view of his disapproval of Rosalind's cigarettes, he opened a concealed cupboard, took from it a box, and selected a long, slim cigar.

Having lit it, and catching her eyes on him, he said, 'I allow myself one of these a day; it's a Corona *colorado claro*. I don't think you'll find the aroma offensive.'

He sat down on the other side of the room, and crossed his long legs and turned his gaze away from her to one of his paintings. Presently an aroma which she found most agreeable drifted to Armorel's nostrils.

Although he had said he disliked having to sit still, for the duration of the concerto his only movement was the rise and fall of his arm when he put the cigar to his lips.

She, when it came to the final movement of the concerto, unconsciously slipped off her shoes and drew her feet up underneath her. Her elbow on the arm of the chair and, her chin cupped comfortably in her palm, she listened, absorbed, to the music last heard on the island which now, in retrospect, seemed more like a prison than a home. Yet, at the time, she had not been discontented there; only vaguely restless sometimes.

When the Rachmaninov concerto ended, Sholto rose and selected another record from a collection of several hundred housed in sliding drawers beneath bookcases matching the panelling, as did the fronts of the drawers.

The next piece of music he played was quite different –

from the concerto for piano and orchestra. It was a light, pretty tune played by an instrument she did not recognise.

'I love that! What is it?' she asked.

'I thought you might like it. It's a Venezuelan waltz for the guitar. The composer is Antonio Lauro, sometimes called the Johann Strauss of Venezuela. He's written a great many waltzes. This one is called *Valse Criollo*, the Creole Waltz.'

He played it for her a second time and, after it, some other pieces for the guitar, but none which she liked as much as the lilting *Valse Criollo*.

It took him about an hour to smoke his cigar, after which he sent her to bed.

'What time have you been having your breakfast?' he asked.

'I used to breakfast at sunrise, but since I've been on board *Isola* Mrs Powers has insisted on bringing it to me in bed about half past eight.'

'Tomorrow you can breakfast with me on deck at seven. Goodnight, Armorel.' He walked to the door and opened it for her.

With a slight sense of being dismissed because he had had enough of her company, she said goodnight and went to her stateroom. As she stepped out of her skirt and put the two silk tape loops in the slots of a skirt hanger, she told herself it was illogical to feel rebuffed at being bade a courteous goodnight when, earlier, she had been in a panic in case he meant to come to bed with her.

Could she believe his assurance that she was safe with him? Somehow she felt that he was a man of his word, but really what did she know about him?

In her bathroom the following morning, Armorel found herself humming the melody of the Venezuelan waltz she had heard the night before. The life-long habit of waking early was still with her, and she had woken at six with plenty of time to bath and dress before joining Sholto at seven. As she lay in her warm scented bath with her knees—rounded again now—making two brown islands in the green-tinted water, she wondered if she would ever become accustomed to the luxury which surrounded her, and if she would miss it when she returned to the ordinary world.

She was ready by ten minutes to seven. When she reached the afterdeck, she found Kit putting the finishing touches to the breakfast table.

'Good morning,' she said, smiling at him. 'I hope you didn't get into trouble after our talk the other day.'

'I did get a bit of a lecture, but old Bates' bark is worse than his bite. I can understand his disapproval. He was trained in the days when everyone kept to their station in life, so the idea of a junior steward chatting up one of the passengers is against his deepest-dyed principles.'

'But you weren't chatting me up—were you?'

He grinned suddenly. 'No, but I'd like to if we weren't where we are, and who we are.'

'But you're not really a steward, and I'm not really a——' She broke off, seeing the change of his expression at the same instant that her ears caught the sound of footsteps behind her.

'Good morning, Armorel. Good morning, Harper.'

Sholto went to the chair in which he had sat the night before, but he did not sit down until Kit had drawn out her chair for her.

'Orange juice for me, please. How do you like to start your breakfast?'—looking at her.

'I'll have orange juice, too, please.'

That Sholto had extremely sharp hearing, and had caught the last part of their conversation, was shown when, Kit having left them, he said, 'You were about to disclaim that you were a passenger, I imagine?'

'I don't feel I am.'

'Your reasoning eludes me.'

'A ... a castaway isn't a passenger, any more than a stowaway. You were forced to take me on board. You didn't invite me.'

'Initially—yes. Not the second time. You're here as my guest.'

'Well, yes, but I still don't *belong* here. Kit Harper is more at home in your world than I am.'

His eyes narrowed slightly; he gave her a long searching scrutiny which she found it quite hard to meet without lowering her glance.

'Did your aunt make you feel that, because your parents weren't married, you were unacceptable socially? If so, she was long out of date. It was the case in her youth, but not today. Our world is not every enlightened, but it is enlightened enough not to hold people guilty for their parents' actions. What are known as one-parent families are a commonplace in our society. Sometimes because a marriage has broken down; sometimes because there's never been one.'

'No, I don't think Aunt Rose ever felt that, or made me feel it,' said Armorel. 'She was not a conventional person, and I'm afraid she disliked all your sex and thought that we—women, that is—were better off without men, except to perpetuate the species.'

'Did she indeed?' he said dryly. 'And was it her plan that you should be the founder of an all-female community, any male children which you produced being dealt with as we're told the Chinese once used to deal with unwanted daughters?'

'Oh, goodness, no! Nothing like that. She knew the world had changed and, had I been as clever as she was.

she would have liked to go back and see me achieve all
the things which she had wanted for herself. She expected
to live at least to ninety, and I think she would have—
but for what happened.'

'Do you feel you can talk about it now? Her letter to
you, which I read, made it fairly clear how your aunt
met her end. But not how the two of you came to be
in that predicament.'

'She died to help me to live,' Armorel said, in a low
tone, looking down at the crisp gingham cloth without
being aware that her fingers were pleating the hem.
'Such fish as we caught, and the rain, was hardly enough
to keep one person alive. So when I was sleeping, exhausted, she wrote that letter and ... gave herself up to
the sea. When I found myself all alone, I almost drowned
myself, too.'

'Which would have wasted her sacrifice. You were
right to hang on. She had had the best of her life. Yours
has scarcely begun,' he said briskly.

Kit came back with two large glass goblets brimming
with chilled unsweetened orange juice. To Armorel's
unsophisticated palate, the refreshing tang of the juice
was more delicious than the fine wine which Sholto had
made her try the night before.

He had liver and bacon for breakfast, while she had a
poached egg on toast as she had several times a week
since being introduced to it on *Isola*.

She could tell from the spread of the yacht's wake,
and a different and stronger vibration in certain parts of
the vessel, that *Isola* was moving at a much higher rate of
knots than before her owner had rejoined her.

'Where are we going?' she asked him.

'To pick up your belongings. You left the bulk of them
on the island where you lived presumably?'

'Oh, yes, because we didn't expect to be away for long.

Or at least Aunt Rose didn't think so. I was worried about our boat. I wasn't sure she was still seaworthy, but Aunt Rose insisted she was. My aunt had become very obstinate in her seventies. It was hopeless to try and change her mind once she'd made a decision. So we set out, and four hours later the weather changed to the storm which blew us off course.'

'What supplies did you have when you started?'

'Some breadfruit and some pumpkins, about half a dozen drinking coconuts, and some cooked fish and taro for our lunch. We also had two gallons of fresh water—more than enough if the storm hadn't come and dis-masted us.'

'So you were short of food and water almost from the outset?'

She nodded, not wishing to bore him by talking too much of their misfortunes. 'It's extraordinarily good of you to suggest going back for our things, but I'm sure it's not worth it. We didn't have many possessions, and nothing of value, nothing I can't live without.'

In fact there was one thing she would have been pleased to retrieve, but if she had learnt anything from her ordeal, it was that no object, however precious, was worth much grief. Life itself was the only real treasure.

'I'm curious to see where and how you lived,' was his answer.

The island, when they arrived there several days later, was as she had left it. No one had been there during her absence, unless the supply schooner had called at last and, finding the two women not there, had gone on her way, her master not troubling himself as to where they might be or whether their absence should be reported.

The one possession which she had felt some sadness at losing was kept in an old biscuit tin. To prevent it being scratched by the other things in the tin, it was wrapped in a scrap of red silk. It was an oval gold locket on a narrow black ribbon. The face of the locket was embellished with a flowing letter A in dark blue enamel and tiny diamond chips, two or three of which were missing.

'What have you there?' asked Sholto, turning from his inspection of the hut which had been their home to see her looking lovingly down at the thing in her palm.

She showed it to him. 'It belonged to my mother's mother who was also called Armorel.'

'Very pretty. You have one or two good pieces here. One wouldn't expect to find a pair of fine old Chippendale carvers on a Pacific atoll, or an antique bookcase.'

'Aunt Rose had them shipped from London. They'd belonged to her parents. I'd better write a note to the trader to say he can take them and sell them, if he wants to. He's bound to call here eventually.'

'No, no, you must keep them,' said Sholto. 'They're handsome pieces of some value, as are these old rugs. They've been badly neglected, but they can be cleaned and repaired.'

'But how can I keep them? I have nowhere to send them.'

'That's no problem. They can be stored in a repository until you want them.' He ducked his tall head to avoid the lintel of the door, and hailed the two seamen with whom they had come ashore.

While his men were transferring her possessions from shore to ship, he and she swam in the lagoon. She had guessed already that he kept himself extremely fit, and although she thought that, in the water, she could probably outswim most of the men on *Isola*, she knew she could not match Sholto who revealed an impressive display of muscle as he stripped off his shirt and trousers. His long legs, too, were well-muscled without being

thick-ankled and furry like those of the two burly seamen in charge of the tender.

As she unzipped her loose cotton sun-dress, Armorel
remembered the way they, and all the other men, had
looked at her in her bikini on the day she had first
talked to Kit; and also the way Sholto had looked at her
on the night when, for the first time, he had seen her
well fed and healthy. Would the sight of her in the brief
two piece rekindle that burning look?

But before she had slipped off the straps and let the
dress slide to her feet on the soft coral sand, he was on
his way down the beach towards the inviting green
shallows.

As she had anticipated, he was a powerful swimmer
and, with his dark hair and tanned shoulders, could have
been mistaken for an islander as he surged through the
water, first in a crawl and then in an equally powerful
backstroke.

They had been in the water for some time when he
swam alongside her, and said, 'Can you swarm up the
palms as fast as the island youngsters do?'

'Yes, I know how to climb the palms. I was taught by
a boy from the schooner when I was little.'

'Show me how it's done, will you?'

'All right.'

They struck out for the beach, and as they waded
ashore she said, 'If you'll wait a minute, I'll run back to
the hut for my climbing ring.'

At the hut she found one of the crew packing books
into stout cardboard boxes. He was there on his own, the
rest of the crew being engaged in taking a load back to
the yacht.

As Armorel entered the hut and reached for the ring
of plaited palm leaves which hung on a peg on the inner

wall, he paused in his task to say, 'Enjoy your swim, love?'

The familiarity surprised her slightly, but she smiled and answered, 'Yes, thank you.'

'I expect when you lived here you bathed in the altogether, eh?'

'The altogether?' she said blankly.

'In the nude.' His pale eyes slid over her body, and somehow he made the word 'nude' sound curiously indecent.

She would have snatched down the ring and hurried away without replying, but the man was holding a book which he must have been looking at because it was open in his hands. As she grasped the ring, he bent it open too far, making the spine crack.

To Armorel, brought up to treat every volume, however shabby, with the utmost care, the sound of the straining binding made her say, 'Oh, do be careful! You'll break the back if you do that.'

'Is this one of your favourites, then?' He turned it towards her, and she saw that it was a book about sculpture, held open at a picture of a statue of a Greek athlete. It was an illustration which she had seen many times before without ever feeling the embarrassment she felt as she glanced at it now, with the seaman watching her, and grinning.

'How about a kiss before you go?' He tossed the book aside, and moved so that he was between her and the hut door.

'Oh, no, please——' she said, in dismay.

'Why not? You'll let him kiss you if he wants, so what's wrong with me? Don't tell me. I'm not a bloody millionaire.' To which he added a remark which, although the words were unknown to her, was clearly a brutal comment on the morals of her sex.

Armorel dodged to the door, was caught by two large sweaty hands, and subjected to a brief kiss; brief because, no sooner had his lips clamped on hers than a cold, incisive voice said, 'Let Miss Baird go.'

The seaman released her at once, and she saw his leer change to a scowl of sullen resentment before, on Sholto's instructions, she left the hut and, trembling, hurried down to the water to wash off the feel of his hands and his horrible mouth.

She was still there when Sholto joined her. He made no reference to what had happened, but said merely, 'Now how about my lesson in palm climbing?'

Although still a good deal upset, she gave him a demonstration of climbing a tree with the plaited palm loop round her ankles to keep her feet from slipping apart and losing their purchase on the trunk.

He acquired the knack very quickly and, answering his questions about the coconut in its various stages of growth, she began, if not to forget her unpleasant experience, to feel less revolted by it.

When they returned to the lagoon beach, after a walk through the groves to the outer beach where the reef was marked by a line of breakers, the Chief Steward had come ashore and set up a lunch table in the shade of a large green sunbrella.

He did not remain to wait on them, but having explained the contents of the several cool bags to her, returned to the yacht with what, she supposed, must be the last load from the hut.

'We're now marooned here till five. I hope, after what happened earlier, the prospect doesn't alarm you,' said Sholto, as they watched the tender leave her mooring.

'No, of course not. Do you ... do you blame me for what happened?'

'Why should I do that?'

'You did warn me that I'd have to learn more discretion than I showed with Kit Harper.'

'That was different,' Sholto replied. 'You had not, I assume, had any previous conversation with that seaman?'

'No, never,' she agreed.

'Commander Watson doesn't often pick a bad lot, but it seems he did this time. The man will be paid off at the next sizeable port.'

'That will make him hate you even more.'

'Hate me?'

'He obviously envies your money and ... all that goes with it.'

'He isn't alone,' he said dryly. 'The world is full of envious people, many of whom could greatly improve their own circumstances if they opted for self-discipline rather than self-indulgence. I've no doubt that man drinks and smokes twice as much as I do. What's left of his pay, he probably gambles away.'

'Yes, but is it quite fair to condemn him on that score? He wasn't born with your intelligence.'

He glanced at her with a raised eyebrow. 'You would defend him, after his barbarous behaviour? You realise that, had you been alone, you might have been subjected to more than a kiss?'

'That was bad enough!' she said, with a shiver of revulsion.

'Had you been kissed before?'

Armorel shook her head.

They were still standing on the beach, watching the tender return to the yacht. Suddenly Sholto took her lightly by the shoulders and turned her to face him. Before she knew what he intended, he put a hand under her chin, tilted her face up, and kissed her briefly on the mouth.

'Was that better perhaps—for a first kiss?' He let her go and stepped back. 'Don't worry: I have no intention of repeating it—or at least not until you're very much older and wiser. Now let's have our lunch, shall we?'

Less than one week later, Armorel found herself sitting in the first class section of a Pan-American Boeing 747, on her way to Paris. She had a seat by a porthole, and for a time she gazed at the ocean thousands of feet below realising, even more clearly than she had while adrift, the vastness of the Pacific.

When the miracle of being airborne for the first time was beginning to wear off a little, she turned her head to watch the pretty stewardesses passing up and down the aisle. Beside her, Sholto was reading a book with, to her, the uninviting title *Hyper-Growth in Asian Economics*. She could tell by the speed at which he turned over the pages that he must have an exceptionally high reading speed, and probably a much greater intensity of concentration than most people, she thought, studying the authoritative lines of his profile.

Since the day they had spent at her island, she had passed a great deal of time pondering what he had meant by saying he would not kiss her again until she was older and wiser. Of the seaman's unwelcome kiss she had thought hardly at all; but every night, before she slept, she remembered Sholto's hands on her shoulders, and the touch of his lips, and the quizzical glint with which he had asked her—*Was that better?*

She had been kissed again before leaving the yacht. Kit, whom she had sought out to say goodbye, had kissed her cheek.

'I'll find out where you are, and look you up when I've finished my stint as a galley-slave,' he had promised. 'Good luck, Armorel.'

While everyone else on the aircraft seemed to spend much of the flight eating and drinking, Sholto ate only salad and drank only water. He did not impose the same abstemiousness on her. 'No, it doesn't matter if you arrive feeling tired, but I spend a great deal of time in the air and it disturbs the system to eat and drink at irregular hours and without any exercise,' he told her.

Every few hours he slept for a time, lying back with his arms folded over his chest and his rather hard face relaxed, although not to the extent of the man across the aisle whose mouth fell open, and who snored and gave restless jerks. Sholto slept heavily and quietly, waking with disconcerting suddenness, and not yawning or stretching but at once re-opening his book, apparently instantly alert.

He did not watch the films, but Armorel gave them rapt attention, never having seen any before. She was too excited to sleep much and, towards the end of the flight, began to feel very weary.

They had fastened their seat-belts for landing when Sholto said to her, 'To avoid the attention of the press, I've arranged for you to be met by Madame Clermont. She's an elderly widow, the mother of one of my French staff. She'll take you to her apartment for the night, and I'll pick you up there tomorrow.' He paused, and she found his expression hard to interpret. 'It's in your own interest that we should appear not to know each other after we leave the plane.'

It was nearly noon the next day when the doorbell rang in Madame Clermont's apartment, and the Frenchwoman said to her guest, 'Ah, c'est Monsieur Ransome qui arrive, je crois.'

Armorel hoped she was right. Kind as Madame had

been to her, she had felt oddly bereft since parting from him at the airport.

Neither of them had had any baggage other than hand luggage, and except for the linen trouser suit in which she had travelled, all the clothes bought for her by Rosalind had been left behind on board *Isola*. However, when she had woken that morning, Madame had produced a pleated skirt and jersey, and a pair of what she called *bas-collants* and which Armorel knew from her recent study of magazines to be known in English as tights. These matched the wool of the skirt and were lace-like in texture with a pattern of diamonds.

'The weather now seems warm to us. But you may feel cold for a time, having always lived in the sun,' the Frenchwoman had explained, when Armorel had looked surprised at being given a pair of tall, soft leather boots to put on over the tights.

Sholto's manner was brisk. Having bade both women good morning, and thanked Madame for her hospitality, he said, 'Are you ready, Armorel? Where's your coat?'

'Oh, the coat! One moment, monsieur.' Madame bustled away and returned with a pale fur jacket with knitted cuffs and a drawstring which gathered the hem close to Armorel's hips. 'And also your bag.' Madame gave her a small skin bag on a long shoulder-strap.

A few moments later, with Sholto carrying her overnight case, they were out in the street, walking to where he had left his car.

The sight of Paris on a fine spring morning kept her in fascinated silence until, on the outskirts of the city, she asked him, 'Where are we going?'

'To the school I told you about.'

'Oh ... already?' she said, rather daunted by the thought of being plunged among strangers so soon after her arrival in this strange new world. As long as Sholto was with her, she felt secure. Without him she had less confidence.

'You'll enjoy it,' he assured her.

Presently she opened the bag and found it contained a silk scarf, a fine lawn handkerchief, a wallet containing French banknotes and a matching purse, a propelling pencil and engagement diary, and a powder case and lipstick.

'Should I put some of this on?' she asked Sholto, holding out the lipstick.

'Why not?' He reached across to turn over the passenger's sun visor which had a mirror attached to the underside.

Carefully Armorel coloured her lips. 'How many other girls are there at the school?'

'Not more than thirty or forty.'

'All French?'

'No, a mixture of many nationalities. French, American, English, Arab ... you won't be the only one adjusting to a new environment.'

'No, but they will know things which I don't—like the name of this lovely fur,' she said, stroking her sleeve.

He gave it a critical glance. 'It's mink—not what I should have chosen, although the style is not bad.'

She said, 'Sholto, what did you mean when you said last night that it was in my interest that we shouldn't be seen together?'

'If we were, it would be assumed that you were under my protection in a different sense from what is actually the case. I prefer you to keep an unimpeachable reputation. If anyone asks you questions, refer to me not by name but as your trustee. Naturally Madame St Cyr, who is the principal of the school, will know how you come to be there, but she is the essence of discretion.'

His car, as she found out later, was a powerful Mer-

cedes coupé which, once they were on an *autoroute*,
purred smoothly along the fast lane until he turned off
at the sign for the small country town where they
lunched.

From there to their destination was less than thirty
kilometres, and Armorel had her first glimpse of what
was to be her new home when they drove down a hill and
she saw the grey, slate-tiled turrets of a small *château*,
its walls and gardens concealed by the pale green spring
foliage of the woods which surrounded it.

Very soon they had swung through its gates and up
the long, tree-lined avenue to a gravel sweep before an
imposing front door.

They were admitted by a maid, and shown to a large
formal salon with silk-cushioned giltwood chairs, a
painted ceiling, and long curtains tied back with cords.
After a few minutes' wait, they were joined by a small
grey-haired woman wearing a jersey and skirt very
much like Armorel's, but with a scarf round her throat
and a brooch to keep it in place arranged in a way which
Armorel saw at a glance was the height of elegance.

This was Madame St Cyr, and after Sholto had kissed
her hand, he introduced them, and the Principal smiled
and said, in perfect English, 'You are rather nervous, I
expect. You have no need to be. You are going to share
a room with another English girl called Jane Bruce, and
she will help you to settle in, and explain anything which
is strange to you.' She turned to Sholto. 'Would you like
to see the house and grounds, Mr Ransome?'

'Some other time, if you don't mind. I have to get back
to Paris.'

'But you'll have some tea before you go?'

'No, thank you, madame. I am en route to New York,
and my flight takes off in three hours. I only stopped
over in Paris to transfer my charge to your care.'

'In that case we won't delay you. I'll leave you to say your farewells.'

'We don't need to be private, madame.' His tone was verging on curtness. He turned to Armorel. 'Goodbye. Whatever you need, Madame St Cyr will procure for you.'

'When shall I see you again?' she asked, as he held out his hand to her.

'I don't know. Not for some time. But you will have plenty to occupy you.'

All too briefly, she felt her fingers gripped in his strong, warm clasp; and then he had turned to the Principal and, shortly afterwards, was gone.

Within a week of her arrival at the Château de Polignac, Armorel felt as if she had been there for months.

Her room-mate, Jane Bruce, was much to her liking; a large, fair, down-to-earth girl who quickly confided that her parents hadn't a bean and her fees were being paid by her grandmother in the hope that she would make a 'good' marriage.

'But I'm afraid she's doomed to disappointment because I shall be just like Mummy and marry for love. That's if anyone falls in love with me. Mummy was gorgeous as a girl, but I'm so huge, and just look at my legs!'

It was true that, as she described them, her legs were rather like tree trunks in the sense of being much the same shape from ankle to knee. But she was so warm-hearted and merry that Armorel felt it would not be long after her emergence from the Château before some per-cipient young man would succumb to charms of far greater importance than shapely ankles.

As well as liking her room-mate, she liked her in-structors, a team of civilised men and women who taught a variety of subjects including *haute cuisine*, needlework, the history of art, current affairs, household management and the principles of interior design.

Sometimes a group of girls would be taken to visit one of the more famous *châteaux*, or a museum or art gallery in Paris. Their curriculum included lectures, concerts, demonstrations of make-up techniques, wine-tastings, coaching in tennis, classes in yoga and many other activities.

In their leisure, although not permitted to leave the grounds without special permission, they were free to stroll in the woods or relax in the comfortable smaller salons, making friends with girls of different nationalities and races and discovering how much, in spite of their cultural differences, they had in common with each other.

When she had been there a month, Armorel was summoned to Madame St Cyr's private sitting-room for what was, Jane assured her, a routine chat about her progress.

It was during this conversation that Armorel voiced what had been on her mind for some time.

She said awkwardly, 'Madame, I should like to write to ... to my trustee, but I don't know his address. Could you give it to me?'

'I can give you the address of Mr Ransome's company office in Paris, and no doubt they would forward your letter. I haven't his private address,' said Madame. 'He left instructions that, in the event of any emergency, we should get in touch with his sister in England. She was a pupil here once. That is how he came to send you here.'

'Oh? Did you know her?' asked Armorel.

'No, she was here in the time of my predecessor. I have been here only eight years, and Mrs Lawrence was here in the late 1960s. It's possible that before I retire her daughters will finish their education with us.'

Later, in their room, Jane said to her, 'You look

rather down. What's the matter? I can't believe Madame harangued you. You're a model inmate.' It amused her to refer to the Château as if it were a penitentiary.

'No, she was very nice,' replied Armorel. 'It ... it's just that she made me think about the future, and what I ought to do with my life.'

This was not the reason why she had come back from the interview feeling 'down', as Jane put it; but it served to cover the real reason—that she did not want a private letter to Sholto to go to his office and perhaps be opened by a secretary.

'I should think you will do what we're all intended to do, won't you?' said Jane. 'Make a so-called good marriage. If any of us were brainy, we'd be at a university, not here. Or I certainly should. But having barely scraped O levels, and with no chance of any A's, I had the choice between getting some humdrum job or taking up Grannie's offer to send me here, and have me transformed into a bride for a duke or a millionaire or, better still, a combination of the two, like Shanaz's brother. But Grannie is rather narrow-minded. East is east, and west is west, and all that. She would draw the line at a sheik's son, even if he did combine the two qualities which *she* considers most important in a husband.'

'I should think kindness is probably the most important quality,' said Armorel, sitting down on the cushioned window-seat and gazing down at the pattern made by the box-hedged beds and gravel walks of the parterre garden on the west side of the Château.

'Yes, that's what Mummy says. Kindness, and a sense of humour. It's nice if they're good-looking, too, but it really doesn't matter a jot as long as they're sweet to you and make you laugh. Grannie says "Nonsense" to that, of course.' Imitating the voice of an elderly woman with a didactic drawl, she said, 'A sensible gel chooses her husband for the way of life he can give her, rather than the man himself. A comfortable home and a good income are far more enduring satisfactions than a few months of being in love.' Reverting to her normal voice, she went on, 'Poor old duck, I don't think she was ever in love. I long for it terribly, don't you?'

'I'm not sure. Yes, I suppose so. If the person I love, loves me. It can't be much fun if he doesn't.'

'That might happen to me. Not to you, with your looks and legs,' was Jane's comment. 'I should think, when you get your discharge, you'll have men swarming round you like bees, unless your old boy makes difficulties.'

Having learned that Armorel was an orphan whose affairs, since the death of her great-aunt, had been in the hands of a trustee, she had jumped to the conclusion that Sholto was a man of advanced years, and Armorel had not disabused her.

'Is that likely?' Jane asked. 'Legally, you're of age now, but perhaps he controls your money until you're older.'

This was a misconception which Armorel would have liked to clear up but how, when she had all the appurtenances of a rich girl, could she explain that, like the other girl's parents, in fact she had not a bean?

Since her arrival at the Château with only the outfit procured for her by Madame Clermont's daughter, and the contents of her overnight bag, her wardrobe had been supplemented by a suitcase full of spring clothes and also the sports kit she needed—a leotard for yoga, tennis dresses and a pale blue track suit.

She said, 'I don't think my trustee will interfere much when I leave here. But my aunt didn't leave me well off. I shall have to work for my living.'

'Really?' said Jane, rather puzzled. 'But you could live for a year on the cost of that blissful fur jacket'—waving her hand towards the long bank of built-in wardrobes on the inner wall of their spacious bedroom. 'Surely the old boy wouldn't have allowed you to buy it if funds were at a low ebb.'

'It was a present from someone, a . . . a family friend.'

Armorel hated being untruthful, but sometimes she found herself in a position where bending the truth was forced on her.

The post reached the Château about noon, and every day she hoped there might be a letter from Sholto. Even a postcard would have pleased her. But five weeks passed and she heard nothing from him.

She told herself it was foolish to be hurt by his failure to keep in touch with her. She should be continually grateful for his lavish generosity; not depressed that, having established her in circumstances of the utmost comfort, he seemed to have forgotten her existence. He was an important and busy man who already had given her far more of his time and attention than she had any right to expect.

One day, in her sixth week at the Château, she was in the teaching kitchen, trying her hand at preparing *truite en colère*, a trout with its tail emerging from its mouth, when Madame St Cyr's assistant entered the kitchen.

'Would you excuse Mademoiselle Baird, monsieur?' she said to the visiting chef who had demonstrated this presentation of the fish to the group with whom Armorel shared her lessons in cookery. 'Madame wishes to see her immediately.'

The Frenchman gave his consent and, wondering what could be the cause of so urgent a summons, Armorel hurriedly washed her hands and took off the overall and the unbecoming but hygienic white cotton mob cap which they all had to wear while cooking.

On the way upstairs, to the Principal's study on the first floor, she remembered that the last time a girl had been sent for in this way, it had been because her father had had a heart attack. Sholto was too young a man for that to be a likely contingency, but could it be—her heart plummeted—that he had been involved in an accident, a plane crash or car smash?

Madame's smiling expression as she entered the study was enough to reassure her that nothing terrible had happened. A wave of relief washed over her.

'An unexpected treat for you, Armorel. Mr Ransome is coming to take you out to lunch. He will be here in fifteen minutes. Unfortunately our telephone line has been out of order this morning, and his Paris office have only just been able to get through to us. However, there's no need to change. Your blouse and skirt are perfectly suitable for luncheon at Le Cheval Rouge which is where I expect he will take you. Just run up and do your hair. It may be that Mr Ransome will wish to have a few words with me before he takes you out. So wait in your room till I send for you.'

Armorel rushed to her room in a fever of excitement. In spite of being told that she need not change, she flung off her blouse and skirt and put on a dress which she thought more becoming and less schoolgirlish. From her room she could not see the drive, nor was there anywhere else from where she could watch the silver Mercedes sweep up to the house. She could only pace about impatiently, wondering if Sholto would find her greatly improved.

At last one of the maids came to tell her she was wanted in the Salon Vert, the beautiful room where they had been received by the Principal on the first day.

Armorel raced down the staircase, but crossed the hall more sedately, inhaling several deep breaths in order to enter the salon looking suitably composed.

But when she set eyes on Sholto, looking even taller and more compellingly virile than she remembered him —perhaps because she had been living in a predominantly female community where the only men she had encountered had been either old, or small and stout— she could not prevent herself smiling a radiant welcome.

'Hello. How are you?' he said.

'I'm very well, thank you. And you?'

'I'm well.' He did not add, as she had hoped he might, 'You've changed. I like the new hairdo.' Although usually so observant, he did not appear to have noticed it.

Madame St Cyr came towards her and, placing her hand on Armorel's arm, said, 'Come, let me present you.'

Only then, for the first time, she noticed there was a fourth person in the salon. A woman dressed in pale grey with a scarlet silk turban hiding most of her hair.

'Madame Lamartine, allow me to introduce Armorel Baird,' said the Principal, leading her pupil towards the chair where the woman was sitting, watching them with eyes as chatoyant as jewels. 'As you would instantly recognise, Armorel, if you had not been in Europe such a short time, Madame Lamartine is one of our most famous film actresses,' Madame St Cyr explained.

'How do you do, Miss Baird,' the vision in grey said graciously.

She was not young, possibly forty and certainly older than Sholto. As she forced her lips into a smile, and made the small bob which the girls were taught to do when presented to people of distinction, Armorel knew, with a curiously painful certainty, that this glamorous woman and Sholto were lovers.

CHAPTER THREE

THE car in which they had come was not the Mercedes but a much larger claret-coloured saloon driven by a liveried chauffeur. Armorel would have been more at ease sitting with him in front, but Madame Lamartine insisted she should come in the back between them. All the way to Le Cheval Rouge she asked her questions about her life at the Château, and about the other girls there. Her interest seemed to be genuine and, had they been on their own, Armorel would have taken it at its face value. But, with Sholto on the other side of her, her answers were stilted. She felt sure he would much prefer to be alone with his beautiful new mistress.

By the time they reached the hotel she had been instructed to call the actress Sidonie. In the women's room, Sidonie did not retouch her make-up, which looked as perfect as if it had just been applied but slipped off the coat of her suit under which she was wearing only a bra of flesh-coloured net appliquéd with what Armorel, having recently heard a talk on the subject, recognised as hand-made lace. The underthings provided for Armorel were pretty, but neither she nor Jane nor, as far as she knew, any of the girls at the Château had a bra which did for their figures what this gossamer garment did for Sidonie. Or perhaps it was she who made it look as if it had been expressly designed for a rendezvous with a lover. Her skin was the colour of cream, with a lovely velvety texture.

She took from her bag a scent spray and puffed a

heavenly-smelling mist all over the upper part of her body.

'Have they taught you to refresh your scent every three hours?'

'No, they haven't told us that.'

'Even in France many women don't scent themselves nearly enough. A little dab behind the ears once or twice a day—what good is that? One must smell divine all the time, and not always of the same scent. Today I am wearing *Opium*. Yesterday, *Bal à Versailles*. But you wear no scent. Why is that? It gives you an allergic reaction?'

'No, I shouldn't think so. I just don't have any,' said Armorel.

The notes in her wallet were still untouched, for although the girls were allowed to go shopping in the small country town which had once been part of the seigneurie of the Château's original owner, it would not have occurred to her to spend the money on anything inessential.

She had hoped that by now Sholto would have found out the exact extent of her aunt's estate, but probably he would not wish to discuss the subject in front of Sidonie. She wondered how much the other woman knew about her background.

The actress had lifted her skirt and was spraying the tops of her thighs. She was wearing fine, pale grey stockings held up by lacy suspenders. Seeing Armorel looking at them, she said, 'I never wear tights. I would as soon wear those long knickers with elastic worn by very old ladies. If a man strokes one's leg, he wants to arrive at bare skin. To find one completely encased in nylon is not at all exciting.' Her strange blue-green eyes sparkled with laughter. 'But of course I am not *une jeune fille bien élevée* being made ready for marriage, and for you perhaps tights are better. You should not allow your legs to be stroked.'

She shook down her skirt and began to put on her coat.
'My youth was very different from yours. I was born in
the slums of Marseille just before they were bombed out
of existence. I had a tough time as a girl, until I caught
the eye of François Lamartine, the film director. He made
me a star, but I paid for it—oh, how I paid for it! He was
a brilliant director, but a beast of a man,' she confided.
'He died about five years ago, and since then I have been
happy for the first time in my life. At last I am independent. I like men, but never again will I let one own
me.'

'Have you any children?' asked Armorel.

'No, thank God! I am not maternal. My work and my
lovers are more than enough to occupy me. Do you feel
you would like to have babies?'

'Not at the moment. But perhaps'—thinking of Jane
—'it's more fun to grow up as part of a large happy
family.'

'But, darling, more often than not these large families
all hate each other. You should only have babies if they
amuse you, and personally I find them boring *au dernier
degré.*'

By the time they had finished lunch, it was not difficult
for Armorel to see what Sholto saw in the actress. She
was outspoken, amusing, exquisitely finished in her person and yet in no way artificial. Armorel longed to be
like her, but knew she had a long way to go to achieve a
tenth part of Sidonie's allure.

It was not surprising that the travelling businessmen
whose cars filled the forecourt and who evidently formed
the bulk of the hotel's midday clientele took as much
interest in her as in their lunch. She had the air of being
a woman who would cater to a man's sexual appetite as
superbly as Le Cheval Rouge catered to his appetite for
food. Armorel felt she would hold Sholto's interest far
longer than Rosalind. He might even fall in love with her,

and want to make her his wife.

After lunch, Sidonie suggested a stroll by the river. She and Sholto walked hand in hand, their fingers entwined. Presently she pulled off the turban which emphasised the beautiful shape of her face, and shook out her hair. It was not the same colour as her dark eyebrows, but a pale ash-blonde mop of curls. Seen from behind, she looked like a young girl. It was only the lines round her eyes which betrayed that she was much older than her figure suggested.

'I've arranged for you to spend the Easter holiday with my sister in England,' Sholto told Armorel on the way back to the Château. 'She has two daughters, a few years younger than you, but they're intelligent girls and I don't think you'll find them uncongenial company. It will give you a taste of English country life.'

She remembered his saying, apropos Rosalind, that he preferred to keep his personal life and his family relationships separate. She, it seemed, was to be counted as part of his family life.

'We'll drop you off at the gates. You don't mind walking up the drive, do you?' he said, as they neared the lodge-guarded entrance to the Château.

'No, of course not. It's very kind of you to have taken me out. It was a delicious lunch, and it's been a great pleasure meeting you, madame,' said Armorel, reverting to formality from a feeling that, in spite of the actress's friendliness, it was proper to show some deference to her.

'And for me, too,' Sidonie said pleasantly.

It would not have surprised Armorel to learn that the outing had been her idea; that, having discovered Sholto had taken on responsibility for a waif and stray, she might have said something like, 'I feel like a day in the country. Let's run down there and take the poor kid out to lunch. If you're her one friend in the world, you ought to spare her an hour or two now and then, darling.'

As they drew up at the gates, the chauffeur pipped the horn twice to attract the attention of the gardener's wife who let visitors in and out. He then sprang out to open the door, and all three passengers got out.

'Back to the nunnery. Never mind: it will not be for ever,' said Sidonie, as the gates were unlocked. 'Au revoir, darling.' She kissed Armorel on both cheeks.

Sholto said, 'Madame St Cyr will be advised about your travel arrangements at Easter. Goodbye. Be good.' He pinched her chin, as if she were the same age as his mid-teen nieces.

'How could she be anything else?' said Sidonie, with her low-pitched chuckle.

Armorel watched them return to the car. As they drove away, Sidonie waved a jewelled hand, but Sholto did not look back.

Why should he? Armorel thought, rather disconsolately, as she thanked the gardener's wife and began to walk up the drive.

Too late, she realised she had forgotten to ask him for an address to which she could write her letter of thanks for the outing. She wondered if his sister would mind having a strange girl foisted on her for the Easter holidays.

The parkland surrounding the pleasure gardens of the Château was grazed by a herd of white Charolais cattle. Half way up the drive, Armorel climbed on the railing which prevented them from straying on to the drive, and sat there for a while, enjoying the solitude of which once she had had too much, and now she had not enough. Much as she liked Jane Bruce, there were times when she would have preferred a room of her own.

Her thoughts returned to the occupants of the gleaming claret limousine, now on its way back to Paris. She visual-

ised them returning either to his or her apartment, and
there making love while the spring day faded into dusk
and the lights of the city came on, and the boulevards
were ablaze as they had been the night she and Madame
Clermont had driven by taxi from the airport to the
Frenchwoman's flat.

With a clarity which caused her a pang of deep unrest,
her imagination projected a vision of Sholto's strong
brown hands peeling off the cobwebby stockings and the
wisps of elegant lingerie until Sidonie was left in nothing
but her delicious aura of *Opium*, ready to be made love
to by a man who, according to Rosalind, was an expert.

Sholto's sister and her family lived in Kent, as did Jane's
parents and it was arranged that the two girls should
travel to Dover together, there to be met by Jane's mother
who would take them to her home from where Armorel
would later be collected by Mrs Lawrence.

The two hours she spent in the Bruce ménage gave
Armorel a glimpse of family life at its best. Jane had not
been exaggerating when she had said her parents were
hard-up. Mrs Bruce, accompanied by two of Jane's three
younger brothers, came to pick them up in an old station
waggon. She was a pretty person, with the taste and style
to wear cheap clothes with an air, but although she was
attractively dressed, she had obviously given up the
struggle to preserve the hands of a woman of even moder-
ate leisure when, as Armorel already knew, her life was
a constant round of kitchen-gardening, baking and cooking, do-it-yourself repairs to a rambling old house, and
expertly tailoring and altering clothes for her beanstalk
sons.

Mr Bruce was an artist who was internationally known
for his beautiful engravings on glass. But although, according to Jane, his work commanded very high prices,

there was a limit to the amount he could do, and his income was eroded by the need for high life insurance to protect his wife who had no career to fall back on if anything happened to him, and by the ever-rising cost of sending three of his four sons to his own old school. Nevertheless, in spite of these financial problems, the Bruces were clearly a united and contented family. As they all sat round the big kitchen table, eating home-made bread with boiled eggs from their own hens, Armorel felt embraced by the affection which flowed between them.

Some hours later, having dinner with the Lawrences in the formal dining-room of their house about fifteen miles away, she could not help contrasting the lively babel of conversation at the Bruce's tea-table with the laconic exchange between her host and hostess.

Mrs Lawrence, who had come to fetch her in a sporty white Citroën, was not much like Sholto in looks except for being rather a tall woman; and, unlike her dynamic brother, she had a rather subdued personality. Her daughters, Melinda and Joanna, were both plump and fair like their father who had come from London only shortly before dinner and, immediately afterwards, retired to his study and was not seen again that evening.

By the time she had been there for a week, Armorel had come to the conclusion that Mrs Lawrence must have married her husband for the reason advocated by Jane's grandmother—because he could provide her with every material comfort, and a house with extensive grounds where, aided by a gardener to do the heavy work, she could indulge her enthusiasm for gardening. Mr Lawrence spent his weekends playing golf, and often he dined in London and did not come home until late. They seemed never to talk to each other about anything other than the headline news and their joint social engagements. They had separate bedrooms and bathrooms, and she never saw them exchange any of the small gestures of affection which she had observed among the Bruces. The thought that she might have to spend all the holidays with them while she remained at the Château had a very lowering effect on her spirits, not only because she was never fully at her ease there, but because she felt sure she must be a burden to them. The girls seemed to like her, especially the younger one, Joanna, but Mrs Lawrence's manner was courteous rather than amiable, and it was not the kind of household where Armorel could make herself useful by helping with the housework and cooking.

One evening, during dinner, Mrs Lawrence said to her husband, 'Sholto rang up today. He's in London for a few days between Gstaad and New York. He's invited us all to the theatre on Tuesday. I told him you had the Institute banquet that night, and would probably sleep at the club, so he's going to drive us home and spend the night here.'

Although she did not show it, Armorel's reaction to this news was an uprush of pleasure as eager as the girl's excitement.

'If we may, we'll go up in the morning with you, Marcus, and the girls can take Armorel sightseeing while I have my hair done,' said their mother.

The thought of the visit to London was the main thing in Armorel's mind throughout the next forty-eight hours. She told herself that anyone would be keyed up at the prospect of seeing a great city and going to the theatre for the first time. But she knew it was really seeing Sholto which made her anticipate Tuesday so impatiently.

Then, on Monday, something totally unexpected and alarming happened.

There was a vanitory unit with a basin in her bedroom,

but she shared a bathroom with the girls. After reading in bed until after midnight, she went to the bathroom and, thinking the household retired, did not bother to put on a dressing-gown over her nightdress. The house was centrally heated, and even at night the temperature never dropped below a comfortable level. Indeed Armorel found it rather stuffy, and usually turned off the radiators and opened her window last thing at night.

Turning the corner where the passage from her room joined the wider main landing, she met Mr Lawrence going towards his room, his footsteps muffled by the thick pile and rubber underlay of the fitted carpet.

'Oh!' With a startled exclamation, she fell back a pace.

'Hello, Armorel.' His voice sounded oddly slurred and, as his gaze travelled downwards towards her bare feet, she regretted having neglected to slip on a robe.

'I'm just going to the bathroom,' she said, instinctively crossing her forearms to cover her breasts, and stepping sideways to hurry past him.

'Oh, don't run away, my lovely.' He caught her and pulled her against him. 'I'll bet *you* aren't a cold fish.'

His breath smelt strongly of whisky, and his kiss was a hateful reminder of the seaman's engulfing wet mouth.

She squirmed and struggled to escape, her disgust mixed with apprehension that Mrs Lawrence might have heard their voices and emerge from her room before Armorel could break free.

Her resistance seemed to inflame him and, when at last she got away, fled to the bathroom and locked the door, one strap of her nightdress had torn away from the yoke, and she was shaking and sickened.

For a long time she did not dare to return to her bedroom. When at last she did unlock the door, the landing was in darkness and as she reached for the switch she was braced for a second attack. To her relief, Mr Lawrence was not lying in wait. Nevertheless, for the first time since her arrival, she took the precaution of turning the key in the bedroom lock.

She was awake half the night, wondering how she could get away from a house where she had never felt at home and where, from now on, she must always be on her guard to avoid being sujected to a repetition of the odious embrace on the landing. That it had been partly the result of his having had too much to drink was not much comfort. He had not been sufficiently tipsy to have, by the morning, forgotten the incident; and she had little doubt that he, like the foul-mouthed seaman, would not take kindly to having been strenuously repulsed.

The next day was far from enjoyable. The girls had different ideas about how best to spend the time before going to their uncle's flat. Joanna wanted to go to the zoo, Melinda to the Tower of London to see the Crown Jewels. To put an end to their bickering, Armorel said she would like to see the British Museum, a suggestion she later regretted as neither of them enjoyed themselves there.

After lunch, at Melinda's suggestion, they took Armorel to look round Selfridges which was not far from Sholto's flat in Avenfield House, a great block of apartments in Park Lane.

Going up to his floor in the lift, Armorel wished she had had the sense to buy a remedy for the headache which had been getting worse all afternoon. She knew it was caused partly by a disturbed night, and partly by being unused to the crowds and the traffic of a capital city. She hoped that she did not look as limp as she felt.

Mr Lawrence had looked rather wan that morning, but her hope that he might be sorry for misbehaving himself the night before had foundered when, during breakfast, he had given her a curiously menacing half-smile which she had read as a signal that, far from feeling remorse, he meant to corner her again.

Mrs Lawrence was already there when the three girls were admitted to the flat by a middle-aged woman in a dark green nylon overall.

Whereas Armorel's skin had been gradually paling since coming to Europe, Sholto seemed browner than ever. She had discovered that the place called Gstaad, where he had been before London, was a fashionable Swiss ski resort where the rich and famous—the girls had mentioned a film star called Elizabeth Taylor,—had holiday chalets. The Aga Khan, Yehudi Menuhin, Julie Andrews and Prince Rainier were some other names they had listed. They had been there themselves the year before, and were disappointed not to have been invited this year.

The reason, Armorel guessed, was because their uncle preferred to have Sidonie Lamartine with him.

'What have you three been doing with yourselves?' he enquired, having greeted them.

Melinda and Joanna told him, and Armorel listened in silence, trying to look as if she were having a marvellous time.

A cup of tea helped to revive her, but although Sholto's housekeeper, Mrs Benson, had provided delicious hot buttered scones, brown bread and cucumber sandwiches, and fruit cake and sponge cake, to which the girls did full justice, Armorel could manage only one scone, and a sandwich which she nibbled with mouse-bites to make it last as long as possible.

They went to the theatre by taxi, with Sholto and Joanna sitting on the fold-down seats facing the other three, one of his long legs almost touching Armorel's. She pretended to be intent on the West End street scene, but by now her temples were aching to an extent which made her dread the evening ahead.

Suddenly Sholto put his hand on one of her knees and said, 'What's the matter, Armorel?'

She considered saying 'Nothing' and smiling, but, after a moment, admitted, 'I have a slight headache. I expect it will go off presently.'

Sholto looked at his sister. 'Have you anything she can take for it? If not, the driver can drop me by Boots in Piccadilly, and I'll walk the rest of the way.'

'But you'll miss the beginning of the show,' Melinda objected.

'No, I shan't. We're in excellent time,' said her uncle.

'I should have some paracetamol.' Mrs Lawrence searched in her bag. 'Yes, here it is. Why didn't you mention you had a headache before?'—as she handed the small bottle of tablets to Armorel.

It was Sholto who answered her. 'Because she's of that increasingly rare breed of person who keep their troubles to themselves.' To Armorel, 'I should have suspected it at tea when you ate almost nothing. Most unlike you. Can you take these things neat? If not, I can get you a glass of water as soon as we reach the theatre.'

'Oh, no, thank you, that isn't necessary. I can swallow them now.' She shook two tablets into her palm, grateful for his perspicacity but hoping he would not divine that she had a weight on her mind which no pills could relieve. If only she could confide it to him! But how could she when the man involved was his brother-in-law?

In the theatre, he sat between his sister and Melinda, with Armorel next to the elder girl and Joanna next to her mother. By the end of the first act, Armorel's headache had cleared and when, on the way to the bar, Sholto asked her if she felt better, she could answer truthfully that she did.

Afterwards they walked the short distance to the restaurant where he had booked a table for supper, returning to Park Lane by taxi to pick up his car which was kept in a basement garage beneath the apartments.

Before they had left outer London, the two Lawrence girls were asleep. In her corner behind Mrs Lawrence, Armorel remained awake, trying desperately to think of a convincing reason for asking Sholto to remove her from his sister's household. She remembered his warning, at the outset of their connection, that she should never attempt to mislead him; but to tell him the truth about her present predicament was impossible.

Now and then, when they overtook another vehicle, and its headlights illuminated the interior of their car, she saw the back of his head with the crisp, clean, well-brushed dark hair just touching the collar of his shirt. Usually he wore rather casual clothes, but tonight he was wearing a suit and a light shirt which accentuated his Swiss mountain tan.

When the road behind them was in darkness, and the car lit only by the reflection of their own headlamps and the faint green glow from the instrument panel, all she could see was the outline of his quarter profile; the high, clever length of forehead between his hairline and eyebrow; the prominent cheekbone above the lean, hollowed cheek, and the strong, clear-cut line of the jaw.

Remembering her view, that morning, of Mr Lawrence's fleshy chin—in spite of his week-end golf, he was not a fit-looking man—she wondered again how Mrs Lawrence could have married him.

Back at the house, the two younger girls were roused from sleep. Yawning and shivering, the night air was chilly after the warmth of the car, they hurried indoors to go straight to bed.

Armorel, having said goodnight to Mrs Lawrence and,

'Thank you for a lovely evening,' to Sholto, would have followed them up the staircase, but he said, 'Wait a moment.'

'Yes?'

'Is there an alarm clock in your room?'

'Yes.'

'Set it for quarter to seven, will you? I want to leave here by eight, but I also want to talk to you, and it's too late for that tonight. We'll meet here at seven o'clock.'

'Very well,' she agreed, somewhat apprehensively.

What could he want to discuss with her? she wondered, as she went upstairs.

He was already in the hall when, on the dot of seven, she went downstairs the next morning.

'It's going to be a hot day. Let's stroll round the garden, shall we? The dew will be heavy still. You'd better do as I have and borrow a pair of Wellingtons from the flower room.'

The flower room was equipped with a sink and a counter where Mrs Lawrence often spent an hour or more creating elaborate floral arrangements for the reception rooms. There was also a row of pegs for mackintoshes, cupboards for sports equipment, and space for rubber boots and other footwear.

Armorel, who was wearing needlecord jeans, stepped into a pair of red rain boots belonging to Melinda. Without socks they were rather too large for her, but would do for a walk round the garden. She also borrowed somebody's old proofed-poplin windcheater to shrug over her lamb's-wool sweater.

They left the house by the garden door, and crossed the large lawn at the rear of the house, leaving two sets of darker green footmarks on the dew-silvered surface of the grass. Compared with the fume-laden atmosphere in

London the day before, the early morning air seemed particularly fresh.

It was not until they reached the path between the tennis court and the beech hedge which screened the kitchen garden that Sholto said, 'I don't think you're happy here, are you?'

'What makes you say that?' she asked.

'When people prevaricate, it's a tacit admission that one's guesswork is well founded,' he said dryly. 'With whom do you find yourself at odds? My sister, or the two girls?'

'I'm not at odds with any of them. Mrs Lawrence and the girls have never been anything but kind to me. But I—I do feel very much an interloper in their lives. If the girls were younger and your sister had no domestic help, I could pull my weight by looking after them, or perhaps cooking some of the meals. As it is, I'm not making myself useful at all.'

They had come to a flight of shallow steps leading down to a sunken rock garden. At the top of the flight Sholto checked and, putting both hands on her shoulders, swung her to face him.

'I don't believe that's enough to make you look as wan as you did yesterday. Yes, I know you had a headache before we went to the theatre, but not afterwards. You don't look bright-eyed this morning. You've changed since I saw you last, Armorel. What's on your mind? Out with it.'

She had a sudden mad impulse to take the single step forward which would bring her close enough to rest her head against his broad shoulder, and there to release the anxiety which had been building up inside her since the night before last. But she knew she must not. Mr Lawrence was Sholto's brother-in-law. She was merely, and temporarily, his dependant.

The shrewd grey eyes looking down at her became slightly narrowed and, it seemed to her, even more penetrating. 'If your problem is not with the distaff side of the family, then it must have something to do with Marcus. Don't tell me he's been fool enough to make a pass at you?'

When he had come so close to the truth, there seemed no point in denying it.

'I—I think it was partly my fault.' She flushed. 'I was on my way to the bathroom, and I wasn't wearing a dressing-gown over my nightie.'

'Good God! Does that excuse him? You're a young girl under his roof. The man must be out of his mind!'

'He'd been drinking,' she said. 'I don't mean he was drunk, but ——'

'What exactly did he do to you?' Sholto demanded.

Suddenly there was on his face an expression of such murderous rage that it frightened her.

'H-he k-kissed me,' she stammered nervously.

'That was all? Nothing more? You're quite certain?' His fingers bit into her shoulders, making her wince.

'That was all. Please . . . oh, *please* don't say anything about it, Sholto. It would be so terribly hurtful to poor Mrs Lawrence if she ever found out.'

'She already knows what he's like. He's been unfaithful to her for years. God knows why she ever married him. Clearly, he married her because she was my father's daughter. I suppose, on her side, it was that dangerous emotion known as being in love,' he said caustically. 'Well, if Marcus's amorous impulses have reached the stage where he can't keep his hands off anyone, the sooner you leave here the better.' He frowned. 'But what the devil am I to do with you?'

'I couldn't come and stay in London with you?' she suggested. 'I shouldn't be a nuisance, truly. I'd be out all day, looking round the museums and art galleries.'

His grim look lightened a little as he said, 'Is that your idea of pleasure? Most girls of your age would rather look round the shops.'

'They're so hot and crowded. I'm still not quite used to the noise and rush of big cities. We went on the Underground yesterday, just from the museum to Marble Arch, and I know it must seem very stupid, but I found it rather alarming.'

They had moved down the steps and were approaching the artificial cascade which was the central feature of the rock garden. The pump which worked it was switched on from the house, and had already been turned on by the woman who came in early to cook Mr Lawrence's breakfast, take up Mrs Lawrence's tray, and vacuum the ground floor rooms. The water was splashing down a series of rocky ledges and making ripples in the pool at the foot of the cascade.

'Not stupid—entirely sensible. The Underground system is Man at his most uncivilised,' said Sholto. 'What is your opinion of this?'—indicating the falling water.

'I think I would rather have a natural stream like the one which crosses the back lane to the village. Have you ever been that way?'

Sholto shook his head. 'I have Claudia and the girls to stay with me sometimes, but I don't come here a great deal. I've never cared for my brother-in-law. Which brings us back to the problem of what's to be done with you. I can't take you back to the flat because I'm leaving at lunch-time, and the place is being shut up for a fortnight for my housekeeper to have a holiday.'

'I'm sure the Bruces would have me, but I couldn't very well propose myself.'

'Who are the Bruces?'

'The people whose daughter is my room-mate.'

Armorel gave him a brief but enthusiastic account of the family and their shabby but welcoming home. The relief of not having to remain with the Lawrences for the rest of the holiday was wonderful, until a fresh worry struck her.

'But even if I could go to them, and I'm not sure they have a spare bed, how can I leave here without your sister suspecting anything?'

He considered this question in silence for the length of a broad path which led between herbaceous borders to her favourite part of the garden, an area of trees and long grass with drifts of daffodils and narcissi growing there.

'Would it make you uneasy to be alone in an hotel in London?' he asked.

'No, I don't think so.'

'In that case I'll tell my sister that, having enjoyed your visit to the British Museum yesterday, you're anxious to see the other museums and it will be more convenient to be on the spot. Claudia is accustomed to my rapid changes of plan. She won't think anything of it.'

'I hope not,' she said uncertainly.

'Run up to your room and pack your things while I have a word with her,' he said briskly.

So it was that less than an hour later she was seated beside him in the car, repeating the previous day's journey but in a much happier frame of mind than the morning before. It was worth the embarrassment she had felt while taking leave of her hostess to know that, with any luck, she would never see Mr Lawrence again.

Whether Claudia Lawrence had swallowed her brother's explanation of why he was taking his protégée away with him had been impossible to tell. She had still been in bed when Armorel had said goodbye, and thanked her for her kindness.

'Not at all. It's been a pleasure to have you,' had been

her response. But her hand had felt limp and boneless in the firmer clasp of her departing guest, and probably she had been saying the customary thing rather than speaking sincerely.

Thinking about the Lawrences' unhappy marriage, Armorel said to Sholto, 'You said earlier, in the garden, that love was a dangerous emotion. Is it always dangerous, do you think?'

'If it clouds the judgment it must be. Alcohol isn't dangerous if it's taken in moderation. In excess, it can be ruination.'

'But can one be moderately in love?'

'Possibly not. I wouldn't know. It's not a condition which has ever, or is ever likely to afflict me. And if I were you, I should steer clear of it yourself—at least for a year or two. To a great extent, your aunt was right. There are better things for an intelligent girl to do with her youth than succumb to the urge to mate—which is what "love" is at nineteen.'

'And what is it at your age?'

'It can be a number of things. In most men, I'd say it's a wish for the greater degree of domestic comfort which a wife will provide even if, nowadays, she's a career-woman. Or if a bachelor life doesn't bother them in that respect, they may feel it would be easier to keep a wife than to have a series of women.'

'You make keeping a wife sound almost like keeping a dog.'

'It's a somewhat similar relationship. Yes, if one considers the matter, a good dog—well-trained, docile, obedient—sets the standard which most men hope for in a wife.'

Armorel gave him a sideways glance. His face was impassive.

She said lightly, 'You must think I'm amazingly credulous if you expect me to rise to that bait.'

A crease appeared in the lean brown cheek nearest to her. It ran from the slant of his cheekbone almost down to the hard knot of muscle which sometimes bunched at his jaw when something displeased him. But the crease, she knew, was the mark of amusement. He kept his eyes on the road and she could not see the warm glint of laughter in them, only the little fan of lines at the side of his eye, and the upward tug of his mouth.

'Yes, I was only teasing you—although not when I advised you to steer clear of youthful infatuations.'

It was a few moments after this that he made room for a driver, who, foolishly overtaking the queue of vehicles in which they were travelling just then, would otherwise have been in danger of colliding with an oncoming lorry.

It so happened that a similar incident had occurred the day before, and Mr Lawrence's reaction had been to close up the gap between his car and the one ahead, cursing the overtaker for his stupidity while being, so it had seemed to Armorel, scarcely less stupid himself.

Sholto's style of driving was quite different from that of his brother-in-law who, once behind the wheel, seemed to hold all his fellow motorists in aggressive contempt. Once or twice he had braked so sharply that the girls had been flung about, and his vituperative comments whenever something kept his speed below sixty had not made for a pleasant journey. With Sholto at the wheel she felt both more relaxed and safer.

That he had a temper he had shown that morning when he had learned of Marcus Lawrence's behaviour to her. But it was a temper well leashed, and not to be triggered by the commonplace irritations of daily life.

He did not, as she had expected, take her to an hotel himself. She was taken to an office and there consigned to the care of a briskly efficient middle-aged secretary.

'I may see you some time next term,' was his casual farewell before he swept out of her life again.

Later, the secretary, Miss Pike, took Armorel in a taxi to the hotel which she had already rung up to reserve a room.

'If you have any serious problems, you have only to ring me at this number, Miss Baird,' she said, jotting it down on an envelope which she took from her neat black calf bag. 'This contains sufficient funds for your day-to-day running expenses until the end of your holiday. You'll find the hotel porter very helpful in advising you how to get about London and what to see.'

Armorel felt that, privately, Miss Pike disapproved of her, and perhaps of Sholto as well.

Her room had a television set. That night she was watching a programme when the bedside telephone rang.

She lifted the receiver. 'Hello?'

'What did you do with yourself this afternoon?'

He sounded as if he were in the next room.

'I thought you were going to New York?' she said.

'That's where I am. The flight takes less than five hours. It's late afternoon here. I thought I'd ring now in case you'd decided to go to bed early. What's that noise in the background?'

'The television. I'll turn it off.' She put the receiver on the bed, and hurried to turn down the sound. When she returned to the telephone the line seemed to be dead. 'Hello? Are you still there, Sholto?' she asked anxiously.

'Yes, I'm here. I was checking another number.'

'You sound so close, and yet you're so far away,' she said wonderingly. Then, remembering his question, 'This afternoon I just wandered about London, exploring.'

'Have you dined?'

'Yes, I went to a nice little snack bar which I found round the corner.'

'You should have dined at the hotel. There's a restaurant there. Didn't you know?'

'Yes, but so expensive,' she objected. 'It was much cheaper at the snack bar.'

'Perhaps, but I'd rather you ate in the hotel. If you're shy of going down to the restaurant, have your meals in your room. The expense is not your concern.'

'But I feel it is. I forgot to ask you this morning if you knew what Aunt Rose had left me.'

'We'll discuss that next time I see you. I'll call you again tomorrow. Goodnight, Armorel.' Rather abruptly, he rang off.

Slowly she replaced the receiver, wondering if the number he had been checking had been Sidonie Lamartine's number in Paris. Probably he knew it by heart and had already called the actress for a long, intimate chat before attending to his duty calls.

The next day Armorel continued her exploration of London; for her lunch buying a packet of sandwiches which she ate on a bench in Hyde Park. To someone accustomed to French bread, the factory bread seemed tasteless, and she fed most of the second sandwich to the sparrows and pigeons.

She was on her way back to the hotel when she thought she heard a male voice call out, 'Hey, Armorel!'

At first, looking round and seeing no one looking at her, she thought she must have imagined it, for who was there who knew her? As Rosalind Plummer had once remarked, here she was like someone from Mars.

Then a taxi, which had stopped to let a car leave a parking space, moved on, and on the opposite side of the street she saw a face which she recognised. It was Ben Bruce, Jane's elder brother who no longer lived at home, but who had been there the day she had met her friend's family.

He crossed to her side of the road. 'Hello! What are you doing here?' he asked, smiling at her.

'Hello, Ben. How nice to see you. I'm staying in London now. I'm not with the Lawrences any more. I—I couldn't impose on them for the whole of the holiday.

'I see. So where are you now?' he asked, taking her by the arm to draw her out of the way of a man who was delivering a trolley-load of cartons to the building by which they were standing.

She told him the name of her hotel, at which he looked puzzled and said, 'You don't mean you're on your own there?'

'Yes, why not? I'm enjoying myself. You take London for granted, but it's new and exciting for me.'

'Oh, yes, in the daytime. But what about the evenings? Do you go to the theatre alone? That can't be much fun.'

'I don't have to go out at night. There's a television in my room, and I have some books to read.' She had them under her arm, having bought them for ten pence each in a second-hand bookshop which she had passed earlier in the day.

Ben took them from her and scanned the spines. One was an out-of-date guide to London, and the other was a novel in French.

'Not very exciting,' was his comment. 'Tonight why not come out with me?'

'I'd like to,' she answered, at once. Then, mindful that he was a student with a grant which would not stretch far, 'But only if you'll let me go Dutch,' having heard of this practice from Jane.

'Okay, if you insist. I have to dash now, but I'll pick you up about seven. Don't dress up too much, will you? A pub supper is about my style at present. The Savoy will come later, I hope, but not till I've qualified. See you!'

With a wave, he went on his way, Armorel watched him for some moments, pleased by this unexpected encounter, and looking forward to going out with him. An instant later she was dashing in pursuit, calling, 'Ben ... Ben, wait a minute!'

'What's up?' he asked, as she caught up with him.

'I forgot—I can't go out tonight. My trustee is going to ring up. I don't know exactly what time, but probably not before nine.'

'Why not leave a message with the switchboard to say you'll ring him back when you get in?'

'No, I don't think I ought to do that. He ... he's rather a stickler for things going according to plan.'

'Then we'll have to make it tomorrow night,' Ben said goodhumouredly.

'Could we? Oh, that would be fine,' she said, greatly relieved.

As Sholto had suggested, that night she had supper in her room. Afterwards she studied the guide book and awaited his telephone call.

Nine o'clock passed, and ten, and as the hands of the clock crept towards eleven she began to fear he had forgotten saying he would call her and that, if he remembered later—for in New York it was still early evening—he might think that she would be asleep.

But as she was beginning to regret that she had given up an evening in Ben's company for a few minutes' long-distance contact with Sholto, at last the set started to chirp.

'What are you watching this evening?' was his first question.

'I'm not. I'm reading.'

'Tomorrow I'll instruct Miss Pike to get in touch with

my bookshop in Piccadilly so that you can buy what you want there, and charge it to my account.'

'Oh but, Sholto, I don't need new books. I'm quite happy with second-hand ones.' She told him about her day, and ended, 'By the way, I met Jane Bruce's brother this afternoon, and he's asked me to have supper with him tomorrow.'

There was a silence at the other end of the line which made her say, 'You have no objection, have you?'

'How old is he? What does he do?'

'I think Jane said he was twenty-two. He's a medical student. He's very like her—oh, but of course you haven't met her. They're all nice, the whole Bruce family.'

'Where is he taking you?'

'I don't know yet. He said something about a pub supper.'

'Well, as long as you stick to wine, and don't let him persuade you to branch into Cuba Libres or Vodkatinis, you should be all right.'

'I shouldn't think he can afford them. I shall probably stick to cokes.'

'Yes, do that, and don't let him keep you out too late.'

Something in his voice prompted her to say, 'Ben isn't at all the wolfish type.'

'Is he not?' Sholto's tone was dry. 'What do you know about that type?'

'Not very much, at first hand, but I've heard the other girls talking.'

'Nothing at all, at first hand,' was his crushing comment. 'And you may take it from a member of the male sex that all men in their early twenties, whether overtly wolfish or not, are bent on bedding as many attractive girls as they can, particularly nowadays when so many of your sex are so readily beddable.'

His tone stirred the latent resentment of masculine

condescension implanted by Miss Rose Newbolt, and made her retort, rather hotly. 'The ones whom you know may be. We aren't all.'

'Your resistance has yet to be tested. Don't make claims which you can't support. I shall ring you tomorrow at midnight. Be there, if you please. Goodnight.'

He rang off, leaving her upset and angry; unable either to concentrate on the novel she had begun, or to settle down to sleep. She accepted that Sholto had the right to dictate her behaviour to some extent, but she did not feel she had deserved the coldly authoritative tone of his final command. She wondered what he would do if she was not in her room when he rang up the following night.

However, her impulse to defy him was only momentary. She was too conscious of being indebted to him for rebellious feelings to last long. As she switched out her light, it was the sense of hurt which lingered; that, and a kind of sorrow that at heart he should hold women in contempt because they gave what he asked of them. She could have understood his attitude had he been old and unattractive, with only his riches to recommend him. But Rosalind had said that she enjoyed being his mistress, and Sidonie Lamartine was wealthy in her own right and could not have embarked on their liaison for mercenary reasons.

Could it be that someone whom he had truly loved had turned out not to care for him, but only for his luxurious life-style? Or was he, like her great-aunt, a being whose emotional make-up lacked the normal person's ability to give and receive affection?

She spent much of the following day at the Courtauld Institute, the art galleries of the University of London, which housed the magnificent collection of paintings made by Samuel Courtauld, one of the last great English collectors with a flair for buying masterpieces by such artists as Cézanne, van Gogh and Gauguin.

She went there partly out of a natural interest in art which had been aroused during her term at the Château, and partly from a wish to please Sholto, also a collector of paintings, by developing a knowledgeable appreciation of them.

She was there until the galleries closed, and then she walked back to the hotel and had a hot bath before dressing in her simplest clothes to go out with Ben.

He took her to a play in the smallest of the three theatres within the National Theatre complex on the South Bank, and afterwards they had supper, not at a pub, but at a cheap but good pizza restaurant.

It was there, while they were both eating a large, bubbling-hot pizza, and sharing a carafe of red wine, that he said, 'What happened to your nails?'

By now, the discolouration of her nails was the only remaining evidence of the privations she had suffered, and soon, because she kept her nails short, even that would have disappeared.

'It—it was caused by a diet deficiency,' she said.

This was an explanation which had satisfied one or two people who had noticed the pale tips of her nails. But Ben, with his greater medical knowledge, said, 'It must have been quite a severe one to have that effect. From the way you're tucking in to that pizza, I shouldn't suspect you of being an anorexia subject.'

'I don't even know what anorexia is.'

'It's an abhorrence of food which sometimes occurs in young girls as the outcome of dieting off puppy-fat; except that, instead of dieting sensibly, they starve themselves and then can't stop. It's a psychosomatic illness which can be difficult to diagnose because people who suffer from it become very crafty at hiding the fact that they aren't eating. A friend of my sister's suffered from it, and it took a long time to cure her.'

'Goodness! How strange,' said Armorel. 'I'm never likely to have it. I love food. I can't resist it. I didn't much like some sandwiches which I bought yesterday—although there was a time when I should have considered them a feast,' she added unguardedly.

A moment or two later, after cutting off another mouthful of pizza, she looked up to find Ben regarding her with a puzzled expression.

'Do you mean you were once short of food?'

'Yes, once—but only for a short time. The ... the island where I grew up was dependent on a supply ship and once, when it didn't arrive on time, our diet became rather restricted.' She hoped this explanation, which was the truth if not the whole truth, would satisfy him.

'Jane told us that you'd been brought up by an elderly relation somewhere out in the Pacific. Are you now quite alone in the world, apart from the old boy you mentioned: your trustee, I think you called him?'

'I suppose I must have some other relations somewhere, but none that I'm in touch with.'

'Very different from us,' was Ben's comment. 'Ma and Pa both come from large families. We have uncles, aunts, cousins galore. Not all greatly loved, I may add. My grandmother who, as probably you know, is paying for Jane to be "finished", is a dragon who terrifies everyone except Pa.'

'My great-aunt was rather a dragon, but in a different way from your grandmother. *Her* ambition, I gather, is for Jane to find a rich husband. My great-aunt's view was the opposite; she abhorred that kind of marriage, or indeed any marriage at all. She thought we should all be careerists and stay single.'

'Is that your view, too?'

'Oh, no, I should like to marry, with a career for a few years beforehand so that it would be there to fall back on later if necessary. The problem is what to do. I don't seem to have a bent. How old were you when you knew you wanted to be a doctor?'

'About fifteen, I suppose.'

Encouraged by Armorel, he talked about his training and his hopes for the future throughout the rest of the meal.

In spite of their agreement the day before, he would not let her share the bill. 'You can ask me in for coffee when we get back to your hotel,' he suggested. 'It's encouraging to see the fleshpots in store for me when I'm a consultant in Harley Street.'

They had coffee in the hotel lounge and, before he left, Ben arranged to see her again the next night. It was only twenty minutes to twelve when Armorel went up to her room. On the dot of midnight the telephone rang.

'Did you enjoy yourself?'

'Yes, very much, thank you. We went to a play, and then to a pizza bar.'

She thought he would ask which play, but instead he said, 'Did he kiss you goodnight?'

'No!' she exclaimed.

'Why not, I wonder?'

'Because he's just being friendly—or don't you believe that people of opposite sexes can be friends?'

'Not unless they're many years older than you and young Bruce, or have had a sexual relationship which has burned itself out. Are you seeing him again?'

'Yes, tomorrow.'

'You can ring me for a change. Have you a pencil to take down my number?'

She scribbled it on the note-pad beside the telephone, and then read it back to him.

'Correct. Goodnight, Armorel.'

'Goodnight,' she echoed, but already the connection had been cut.

She replaced the receiver on its rest, disappointed that their conversation had been so cursory.

The next day, when she returned from a visit to the Tate Gallery, the porter gave her a message from the switchboard when he handed her her room key. Mrs Bruce had rung up and would like Armorel to call her back.

The Bruces' telephone was answered by one of the younger boys, and a few minutes later his mother, rather breathless, came on the line.

'Hello, Armorel. Ben rang up last night and mentioned that you'd been to the theatre together. As I hear you're on your own now, I wondered if you would care to spend the last two or three days of the holiday with us?'

'I'd love to, Mrs Bruce. Thank you. But could I speak to my trustee before accepting definitely? I'm ringing him up tonight, and could call you back early tomorrow.'

'Yes, do that. I won't put Jane on the line because she's a terrible chatterbox, and you can exchange all your news when you see each other. Goodbye, my dear.'

That night Ben took her to supper with a fellow student called Sammy and the girl-friend with whom he shared a flat. Sammy's girl, Liza, had cooked a large dish of moussaka which they ate with a bottle of what they called supermarket plonk. To Armorel, it tasted excellent. She wondered what Sholto would have made of it, and of the cluttered studio flat.

When she rang him that night he was out. She left a message with the American operator to tell him that she had called at five minutes past twelve.

At noon the next day she called the number again. This time the operator did not tell her that Suite 16 was not answering. But the next voice to come on the line was not Sholto's. It was feminine and drowsy.

'Oh, I'm sorry. I think they must have put me through to the wrong extension,' Armorel apologised. 'I wanted to speak to Mr Ransome.'

'He's right here. Who wants him?' enquired the sleepy female voice.

'Armorel Baird.' Even as she gave her name, she knew she had called at a singularly unsuitable moment.

Whoever was at the other end did not trouble to cover the receiver as she called in a voice intended to carry some distance, 'There's a girl on the line for you, honey. Somebody Baird. I couldn't make out her first name.'

The next voice was Sholto's, curt with annoyance. 'What the devil are you doing, ringing me up at this hour?'

'I wanted to catch you before you went out for the day. How was I to know you'd be in bed with one of your ... your popsies?'

It was an expression she had picked up from Ben and his friends who had used it to refer to the mistress of a well-known actor.

'I'm not in bed. I'm shaving. I was given your message last night. What do you want now?' he asked coldly.

'Your permission to spend the last two or three nights of my holiday with Jane Bruce and her family.'

'By all means. Is that all?'

'Yes, thank you.'

'Then I'll carry on shaving. Goodbye.'

She replaced the receiver, knowing that he was very angry with her. But why, when he had made no secret of his two previous liaisons, he should be angry now was something she could not understand.

CHAPTER FOUR

IT was the last contact she had with him during the holiday. He did not telephone her again, and she did not dare telephone him. That she had incurred his displeasure cast a shadow on her enjoyment of her stay with the Bruces.

The day before she and Jane returned to the Château, Mrs Bruce asked Armorel if she would like to stay with them again during the month which they spent every summer on the island of Alderney.

'One of my husband's uncles left him a house there which we use ourselves for four weeks, and let for the rest of the summer,' she explained. 'You're more than welcome to join us, if you would care to.'

'Do come, Armorel. You can help me redecorate my room,' said Jane.

'I should love to come,' Armorel answered.

'Then if you'll give me his address, I'll write a letter to your trustee. As he hasn't met us, a formal invitation is indicated,' said Jane's mother.

'He ... he isn't in England at the moment. I'm not quite sure where he is. But Miss Pike, his secretary, will know. You could write to her, Mrs Bruce.'

'And what is your trustee's name?' asked her hostess, when she had made a note of his secretary's name and the address of Sholto's offices in London.

'Ransome ... his initial is S,' Armorel said reluctantly, mindful of Sholto's warning on the day he delivered her to the Château.

Fortunately the name did not seem to ring any bells

with the Bruces, and it was not until later that Armorel
began to have second thoughts about the wisdom of
accepting their invitation in case it conflicted with
Sholto's summer plans for her, and meant she would see
less of him.

Within a fortnight of their return to the Château, Mrs
Bruce wrote to her daughter that not only had Mr Ransome no objection to his charge going to Alderney with
them but that, afterwards, in return for their hospitality
to her, he hoped the Bruces would allow Jane to accompany Armorel on a visit to a villa in Tuscany where they
could explore the delights of that lovely part of Italy.

For two of the four weeks they spent on Alderney, Ben
was there and, with him, Armorel experienced for the
first time the pleasures of a lighthearted holiday romance.

On his last night he hinted that, on his side, their summer idyll could grow into something more serious and
lasting; but she knew that, for her, Ben could only ever be
a friend with whom she had shared a few tender moments
and goodnight kisses. She chose not to examine the reason why she felt so certain of this. Although she missed
him slightly for a few days after his going, the little island
retained its charm for her and the hours were not long
and empty without him, as she felt they must always be
when a man whom one truly loved was no longer present.

Two days after the family's return to Kent, the girls
flew to Italy.

'Goodness, what luxury!' exclaimed Jane, when they
were met at the airport by a large car driven by a chauffeur. 'I'm sure you must be holding out on us, and you're
really an heiress to an incredible fortune.'

'I can assure you I'm not,' said Armorel. 'Perhaps
Signora Toscari is.'

This was the name of the woman who was supervising
their visit and who, about an hour later, welcomed them

to the Villa Contenta, a sixteenth-century country house surrounded by vineyards and low cypress-shaded hills.

Jane assumed that Signora Toscari was the owner of the villa, but Armorel suspected that it belonged to Sholto, and that the Italian woman was a kind of superior housekeeper. She had not seen Sholto since the spring, but had received a long, businesslike letter from him in which he had explained that most of Miss Newbolt's income had derived from an annuity which had died with her. With Armorel's authority, he proposed to re-invest her great-aunt's other assets to greater advantage than had been the case in the past. In the meantime he hoped she would accept from him such assistance as might be necessary until she reached her majority, by which time her present resources should be substantially improved.

It seemed to Armorel that even a financial genius, which presumably Sholto was, would never be able to transform a few hundred pounds into the many hundreds necessary to repay him properly. She had written her reply, accepting his continued help, in a very uneasy state of mind; feeling that it was not right to let him provide for her, yet fearing that, if she insisted on standing alone, she might never see him again.

Throughout their sojourn in Italy she hoped that, despite Jane's presence, he might pay a flying visit. But the hot days and balmy evenings passed without any sign of him, until brown and, in Jane's case, several pounds plumper, they returned to England for the last few days before the autumn term began.

It was not until Christmas that Armorel saw Sholto again. A week before the girls dispersed to their homes, she received a letter from Miss Pike, instructing her to go to Switzerland and enclosing tickets and a cheque to be cashed by Madame St Cyr to cover the cost of ski clothes and ski classes.

Full insurance has been arranged and Miss J. B. Lister,

who is in charge of the chalet, will advise you on the necessary clothing and equipment, wrote Miss Pike.

It would have been friendly, thought Armorel, to have added some brief personal postcript such as 'Have fun'. She hoped Miss J. B. Lister would not prove to be as unbending as Sholto's secretary. Would he be there? Perhaps not. Anyway it would be fun learning to ski, and no doubt she would quickly make friends.

To her relief, almost the first thing Miss Lister said, when they met, was, 'Call me Jilly. Everyone does.'

The first thing Armorel wanted to ask was, 'Is Mr Ransome coming?' but she reserved this question until after their arrival at the largely timber-built chalet with its overhanging snow-capped eaves and several carved wooden balconies.

'Yes, he arrives on Christmas Eve with a party of ten, making twelve in all,' Jilly told her, as she showed her upstairs to a cosy pine-panelled bedroom with a view over sparkling white snowfields patched with dark green forest.

Next morning she took Armorel shopping, advising her to buy first an all-in-one quilted buttercup yellow ski-suit which zipped apart to form an anorak and pants, and also had zip-off sleeves which turned the top into a gilet to wear over a sky blue sweater and matching padded pants.

In addition to these outer garments, she needed cotton long johns and polos, flow ski boots, middling length skis, goggles, leather gloves with silk lining gloves, and thin woollen socks.

'And you'll need what's known as a bum-bag for your money and make-up,' said Jilly. 'If you put things like that in your pockets it spoils your shape, which would be a pity when you have the kind of shape which looks good even when padded.'

The bum-bag strapped round the waist and rested in

the small of the back, and the final piece of equipment was an *abonnement*, a season ticket with Armorel's photograph on it which she wore on a chain round her neck and showed when she wanted to use a ski-lift without having to fumble for coins.

For three days Jilly, an expert skier, gave Armorel private coaching, and then it was necessary for her to concentrate on the preparations for the arrival of Sholto and his guests. Thereafter Armorel joined a class taken by a good-looking blond *lehrer* who flirted with all his women pupils, but whose merry blue eyes had no effect on her because she could hardly wait to see someone with dark hair and grey eyes, even though she didn't expect him to take much notice of her.

On the morning of Christmas Eve, she shared an anchor tow with a young man wearing a bright red version of the dungarees-style garment she had heard called a *salopette*. She had been told that the anchor was the most difficult type of lift for a novice to master, and was rather nervous of falling off it and having to return to the end of the queue.

Fortunately he didn't attempt to chat her up, but left her to keep alert for the sudden jerks and awkward patches of hardened snow about which she had been warned. Also, apparently, it could be dangerous to let go of the anchor too soon. It had to be allowed partially to recoil.

Her arrival at the top safely accomplished, she heaved a breath of relief and would have murmured a polite '*Au 'voir*' had not her tow partner said in English, 'Haven't we met somewhere before?'

It was such a hoary gambit that she would have smiled and pretended to speak only French, but just then the young man removed his goggles and she recognised him.

'Kit ... Kit Harper!'

'I know I know you, but I still don't know who you are. Take off your goggles,' he suggested.

Her hair was tucked inside a woolly cap. She lowered her goggles and let them hang round her neck. She had been protecting her skin from sunburn with a glacier cream recommended by Jilly. Now, after a week of mountain air, sunlight, early nights and strenuous exercise, she knew she had never looked browner or healthier.

For a moment he still didn't recognise her, and then he exclaimed in astonishment, 'Good God! It's Annabel! I've often wondered what had happened to you.'

'Armorel . . . Armorel Baird,' she corrected.

'Oh, yes—sorry. Slip of the tongue.'

She smiled. 'It's been a long time. I'm surprised you remember me at all.'

'How could I forget?' His eyes swept the slender form which even a layer of quilting could not disguise. 'What a marvellous stroke of luck—especially if you're alone, too.'

'I am at the moment. Are you here with your family?'

He shook his head, and explained that he had come with a party of young people who were staying in a chalet belonging to the parents of one of them. The girl who was to have been his skiing companion had been taken ill at the last moment, leaving Kit an odd man out in a group of pairs.

'Not that I knew her very well, so it wasn't too much of a disappointment. But I didn't expect to run into someone I did know—someone five times as dishy as Sue—on my second day here.'

'Ah, but I'm only a beginner on skis, and you look as if you might be an expert,' she said.

'Not an expert. I've been skiing since I was small. How much of a beginner are you?'

She told him, and guessed that he had to repress a grimace of dismay. But when he had seen her in action, he said, 'I can't believe you've been skiing for less than a week. You must be a natural. With practice, you could be good.'

Knowing how busy Jilly was, Armorel had said she would have her lunch in a café. Instead, Kit took her back to the chalet he was sharing, and introduced her to some of his friends.

Earlier, they had brought each other up to date with what had happened to them since their last meeting, and, before she met his companions, Armorel had asked him not to mention her connection with Sholto to them.

'Still keeping you under hatches, is he?' had been Kit's comment.

'Yes, he is. I'm not one of his girl-friends, and I suppose he doesn't want people to jump to any false conclusions.'

'How odd. That, in all this time, he's never made a pass at you.'

'I've hardly seen anything of him—not since last spring, in fact. Anyway, Sholto isn't a rip-roaring wolf as some of the ski *lehrers* are said to be.'

'Is yours?' he asked, grinning.

'Yes, but not with me. My class is full of eager females, but I'm not one of them.'

She was not too sure that she liked Kit's friends who were mostly in their middle twenties and all, to use Jane's mother's term, rather hard-boiled types, or so they seemed at first meeting.

Had she not met Kit, instead of skiing after lunch she would have returned to the chalet to be there when Sholto arrived. But Kit pointed out that the house party might not turn up until late—as in fact she herself had done—and she might as well ski with him as hang about wasting an opportunity to practise.

So the bright day was fading into dusk when she tramped home and, seeing every room in the chalet alight, knew that Sholto and his friends were there before her. Pulling her bag round to the front of her, she quickly applied some lipstick, and took off her cap to run a comb through her hair.

She was in the hall, taking off her boots and listening to the buzz of voices from the large, lofty sitting-room which had a gallery all round it leading to the first floor bedrooms, when Sholto himself came down the open-tread staircase.

'Hello. Have you been enjoying yourself?'

'Hello. Yes, I'm having a lovely time, thank you.'

He crossed the hall to her side, and she stood up to take off her anorak. He seemed even taller and broader than she remembered.

As he pinched her cheek, he said quizzically, 'Is that glowing look all due to exercise, or could it be that, like thousands of others before you, you've taken a shine to your *lehrer*?'

He spoke, she thought, as to a girl of sixteen. 'No, only to exercise. My *lehrer* is very dashing, but not my type.'

'Oh? What is your type?' he asked, amused.

Armorel wondered how he would react if she had the boldness to answer 'You are'. Instead she said, 'Guess who I met on the anchor tow this morning? Kit Harper. Do you remember him? He's the son of a friend of your sister's. He was working as a steward on *Isola* at the time you rescued me.'

'And he is your type, hm?'

'I don't know. It's too soon to say. Perhaps,' she said airily.

'Come and meet the others.'

'Could I have a shower and change first?'

'Of course, as you wish. See you later.' He turned away to join his friends, leaving her feeling deflated.

It had not been the meeting she had looked forward to, and she wished she had not mentioned Kit and implied an interest in him which did not exist.

Sholto was deep in conversation with a stylish brunette when, half an hour later, Armorel paused in the sitting-room doorway, looking at the people assembled there.

At first none of them seemed to notice her, and she felt rather shy of going among them. But then an elegant woman rose from one of the sofas and came towards her, smiling.

'I'm Ellen Bocage ... an American by birth, and French by marriage. How do you do, Miss Baird? Come and meet my family.' She introduced her husband, Adrian, her married daughter Marie-France and her husband Pierre, and two teenage boys, one called Scott and the other Charles, although he was always known as Chuck.

The four other people present were an elderly couple, John and Edwina Hammond, who did not ski but liked to skate, and an unattached man, Hal Lake. The brunette was Diana Marshall whom, judging by the way she had seen him smiling at her, Armorel took to be Sholto's latest amour.

During the day a large Christmas tree had been raised in a corner of the room and, after supper, Marie-France and Armorel and the two boys decorated it with baubles and strands of tinsel from a box kept from year to year. Jilly, who had been Sholto's chalet girl for several seasons, had told Armorel that it was usual for all the Christmas presents to be placed beneath the tree, and not opened until after dinner on Christmas night, most of the day being spent skiing. Armorel's present for Sholto was something she had organised in Paris at half-term while she had been there as the guest of a French friend. Her presents for the others were small things she had bought in Gstaad since her arrival.

The Hammonds retired to bed early. Everyone else stayed up later, eating hot mince pies, and drinking the hot, fruity, spicy punch known in the mountains as *glühwein*.

It was Christmas Eve as Armorel had often imagined it; the distant snowfields and high peaks glistening coldly under the moon, the lighted windows of the other *schalis* glowing more warmly by contrast, a record of carols from King's College Chapel on the music deck, the resinous scent of the pine branches emanating more strongly in the warmth of the central heating which made the log-burning stove a pleasing accessory rather than a necessity, and everyone in a happy, festive mood.

She said goodnight and went to bed at the same time as the two boys and their parents. But Marie-France and her husband, and Sholto and the two others, remained downstairs.

Usually Armorel fell asleep within seconds of closing her eyes. But tonight, in spite of several glasses of *glühwein* in addition to the soporific effect of a day's skiing, she found herself wide awake.

She had been in her room about an hour, and had given up trying to read but was still sitting up in the dark, looking out of the double-glazed window, when the door was opened and someone came in. As he passed the window she recognised Sholto's tall form, and said, in a startled whisper, 'Is something the matter?'

'You should be asleep. Why aren't you?' he asked, in a voice not as hushed as hers, but low enough not to be heard beyond the bedroom.

She reached out to switch on the lamp, and saw him standing by the foot of her bed, one hand thrust into the pocket of a dressing-gown of dull black silk piped with grey silk, and the other behind his back.

'I don't know. I'm just not sleepy.'

'Well, I am, and I don't feel my role as Father Christmas requires me to stay up any later than this,' he said dryly. 'I had a telephone call from your friend Jane Bruce a few days ago. She wanted to know if I should be seeing you at Christmas. When I told her I should, she came to the office with this, which I was instructed to hang on your bedpost at dead of night.'

From behind his back he produced a red felt stocking ornamented with red and silver sequins, and bulky with packages.

'She said you'd never had one before. It was supposed to surprise you when you woke up, but I suppose now you won't be able to resist opening it at once,' he said, with a smile, as he laid the stocking in her lap.

Armorel looked at it speechlessly for a few moments, her eyes glazed by sudden tears.

'H-how extraordinarily kind of her,' she said huskily. 'No, I never have had a Christmas stocking before.'

Blinking, she began to open it, and Sholto sat down on the bed and watched her take out the parcels which were intermingled with tangerines, walnuts, little packets of chocolate drops, and a huge white sugar mouse which Armorel guessed was one of a litter of mice made by Jane's mother for the stockings which all the Bruce children always received every Christmas, even when they reached Ben's age.

She had unwrapped only one of the parcels—an initialled key ring from Timmy Bruce—when Sholto said, 'Perhaps a cup of hot chocolate would settle you down for the night. I'll go and organise it.'

'You're not going to wake up Jilly?' she asked, as he rose.

'My dear girl, do you think me incapable of something as simple as making chocolate?' he returned, with a lifted eyebrow.

By the time he reappeared, she had opened all the little packages and arranged them, with their cards, on the dressing-table. She was climbing back into bed when Sholto re-entered, carrying a mug with a wisp of steam rising from it which he set on the glass-topped night-table.

'So you've met Jane?' Armorel said.

He resumed his seat on the bed. Under the dressing-gown he was wearing pale grey pyjama trousers but not, apparently, a jacket. His brown chest was bare where the front of the dressing-gown fell open.

'No, I wasn't there when she delivered the parcel and the note which accompanied it. I had a few words with her on the telephone when Miss Pike, rather reluctantly, put her through to me.'

'Your voice will have given away that you aren't the white-haired old fogey the Bruces have always imagined.'

'Not necessarily. Voices can be misleading. Here's a stocking filler from me,' he said, taking a parcel from his pocket, and tossing it to her. 'There's another present under the tree for you, but that's a little something I picked up yesterday. I thought it was rather your style.'

The parcel was long and thin, suggesting it might contain a pen. But the paper wrapped a box with a slim leather case which, opened, revealed a delicate bracelet formed by six tiny, exquisitely carved cameos, each one linked to the next by several strands of the finest possible gold chain.

'Oh, Sholto! It's perfectly lovely!' She took it carefully from its bed and laid it across her left wrist.

He leaned forward to fasten it for her. 'Yes, it suits you. I thought it would. You have pretty wrists,' he said casually.

'Have I?'

She had never studied her wrists, and was surprised that he had.

On impulse she scrambled into a kneeling position and, with her hands on his shoulders, planted a hearty kiss on the lean dark cheek nearest to her.

'Thank you—and a very merry Christmas to the kindest and best of "trustees",' she said warmly.

His strong hands closed on her waist, making her suddenly aware that although her nightdress, made of an olive green Liberty print, was not transparent, the cotton voile was very thin, and the style quite low-cut. A demurely high-necked winter nightie would have been too warm in the chalet's level of central heating.

She sank back on her heels, her hands sliding down from his shoulders to rest on the powerful chest muscles under the expensive black silk. For a moment she thought he was going to return her Christmas kiss, and not on the cheek but where he was looking—at her lips. His hands seemed to draw her towards him, and she would not have resisted their pressure, but he changed his mind and said, with a look of amusement, 'I think you've had a little too much *glühwein*, my girl. Drink your chocolate and go to sleep. We don't want to be too tired to enjoy tomorrow's skiing. Goodnight. Happy Christmas.'

It was half past nine before Armorel woke up on Christmas morning. When she went downstairs, everyone but Jilly had gone out, so she stayed to assist the older girl with her preparations for lunch. Sholto, it seemed, had not overslept as she had, but had been the first to go out, so perhaps he had not gone from her room to Diana Marshall's, as she had wondered if he might have done.

At one o'clock everyone assembled for a glass of champagne and a light lunch outside on the largest balcony. Sholto was wearing a scarlet racing *salopette* over a thick black sweater. With the aid of field glasses, Armorel had watched him and Diana on their final run down within sight of the chalet. Jilly had pointed them out to her as they snaked their way down one of the fastest pistes, sometimes in sweeping traverses, lovely to watch, and sometimes headlong down the fall-line, a term which Jilly explained as the steepest way down a slope.

'Mr Ransome could have been an Olympic skier if he had more time for it,' said Jilly.

Armorel remembered this remark when, as luncheon was ending, he suggested they should all change partners, with Diana going with Hal and Armorel coming with him.

'Oh, no, I couldn't ski with you. I've hardly begun,' she protested.

'That's okay. I'll give you a lesson.'

They were sitting next to each other, and as she opened her mouth to express a further objection, she felt his knee nudge against hers under the gingham-clothed table and saw in his eyes a meaning look—though precisely what the meaning was she could not be certain.

He explained it later when, side by side, they were soaring upwards in a chair-lift.

'I have a particular reason for wanting Diana and Hal to ski together as much as possible. They've both been through a bad time. Diana's husband was killed when a terrorist bomb blasted a building a couple of years ago, and about the same time Hal's wife left him for another man. Since then he's divorced her, and I think he and Diana are ready to make a fresh start, and might make it together.'

The discovery that he had no personal designs on Diana had a more euphoric effect on Armorel than the glass of champagne before lunch. 'I shouldn't have suspected you of being a match-maker, Sholto.'

'I'm not, and nothing may come of inviting them here to meet each other. But they both fitted in with the kind of quiet family party I wanted to have here this Christmas.'

'What kind of parties do you usually have?'

'Orgies,' he said, with a mocking look. 'Not for people of your tender years.'

'I have been out in the world for quite some time now, you know.'

'Yes, but always under the wing of Madame St Cyr, Signora Toscari or your friend's mother. I think you need more time yet before you qualify for complete self-possession. How is your Italian now?'

For the rest of the ride he talked to her in that language, and seemed pleased with her greater fluency since her stay at the Villa Contenta which, as she had surmised, did belong to him.

He was also impressed by her aptitude for skiing. But when, in an effort to make herself less of a drag on him, she flung herself down a fall-line, she ended up on her back with her skis and poles in the air.

'You'll be going down on the blood wagon if you do that again,' said Sholto, helping her to pick herself up, and dusting her down.

'I'm sorry,' she said, much mortified. 'I knew you shouldn't have brought me. I should have gone with the boys.'

'Those two harum-scarums wouldn't have looked after you. You'd have got left behind, had a fall and then I should have had to come looking for you.'

He was dislodging the snow from her suit with light patting movements with his open palm and, even through his leather glove and her layer of padding, she was intensely conscious of his touch.

'From now on take it easy, if you please. Pluck is no substitute for technique, and you don't want to start the New Year with a pin in your leg and only a good book for company,' he said, when he had finished with her. 'But pluck, if it isn't too reckless, is a very desirable characteristic,' he added, with a sudden grin which made her feel that perhaps she hadn't made a complete fool of herself.

Later, dressing for dinner, Armorel felt it was too much to hope that he would take her skiing again. But it had been a lovely experience to wing gently down the mountain with the snow-laden branches of the spruces glistening in the afternoon sun, and every so often a stop for him to admire the view and for her to steal covert glances at the hawk-like profile and glossy dark hair of her companion. In the morning, both he and Diana had skied in helmets. But in the afternoon he had gone bare-headed, and with wind-ruffled hair he looked more approachable and less the worldly tycoon to whom all women were merely toys.

All the girls at the Château had to have one formal evening outfit, and Armorel's was a short dress of ochre crêpe-de-chine with narrow shoulder straps holding up a low-cut top, a tight waist and a full skirt. With it went a jacket of the same material printed with flowers in khaki, violet and pink, their outlines quilted. That night she wore it without the jacket and with Sholto's cameo bracelet on her wrist. Although he had spoken as if it were an inexpensive trifle, inside the lid of the case the name of a famous Bond Street jeweller was stamped in gold on the white satin lining.

At dinner she sat between Monsieur Bocage and his son-in-law. The Bocage boys acted as waiters under Jilly's direction and when each course had been served she, looking very attractive with a ruffled black broderie anglaise pinafore over her black cashmere dress, took her place at the table with everyone else.

The meal began with little puff pastry tartlets filled with smoked salmon, followed by a large roast goose stuffed with prunes and surrounded by spiced apples. Later, for those who wished for something lighter than the traditional plum pudding and brandy sauce, Jilly had made a strawberry soufflé.

It was nearly eleven o'clock before the ceremony of opening the presents began. To her surprise and pleasure, Armorel found that everyone had come with a gift for her in their luggage. They must have been told beforehand that she would be present. Soon she had more than one bottle of scent, silk scarves by Jaeger and Liberty, a drum of French talc, a diamanté hair-slide and many other nice things ranged on the floor by her chair.

Her second present from Sholto was one which those who did not know about the cameo bracelet might have thought somewhat disappointing for her. It was one of the classic cookery books, and in fact she was glad to have it.

Her present to him was one of the last to be opened, and she watched with considerable tension as he stripped off the wrappings and uncovered the small watercolour sketch by an artist she knew he collected, and which she had happened to notice in an open portfolio of drawings in a gallery in Paris where she and her French friend, Louise, had been waiting for Louise's mother to choose a frame.

He crossed to where she was sitting. 'Where did you find this, Armorel?'

'In a back street in Paris,' she answered, not entirely untruthfully, since the gallery, though famous, was not on a main boulevard. 'Of course it may not be genuine. Perhaps the initials are a forgery.'

'I think not. And you've had it framed to match the

others I have. Very sharp of you to remember how they were done.'

'I particularly liked them,' she said lightly, having often studied the group of the artist's larger, finished pictures during her time on board *Isola*. The work she had given to Sholto was only a preparatory sketch. Even so it had been expensive, and she had not bought it with his money but with her own, in so far as she was entitled to call any money her own when she knew that the dress she was wearing must have cost him at least half as much as the cost of the picture.

'Thank you. I don't know when I've had anything which has pleased me more,' he said, looking down at her with a seriousness which gave her the delighted conviction that he meant it.

'Or I,' she murmured, touching her bracelet.

A shriek of joy from Marie-France distracted them. The Franco-American girl had unwrapped a large box and found in it a white mink jacket which, when she had put it on, caused her to fling her arms round her young husband's neck.

The evening ended with dancing, and Sholto was dancing with Armorel when, to her vexation, they were interrupted by a loud rapping on the front door.

'Who's our caller, I wonder?' he said. 'Excuse me. I'll go and find out.'

She followed him to the threshold of the sitting room and, when he opened the door, saw Kit in the lobby.

'Good evening, Mr Ransome. I hope I'm not intruding. I wanted to deliver a small Christmas present to Armorel.'

'Not at all. Come in. Have a drink,' said Sholto.

'Thank you ... just for a short time. I could do with a tot of something. It's a lot colder out at night.' As he began to shed his outer garments, he noticed Armorel in the doorway, and said, 'Merry Christmas.'

'Merry Christmas,' she echoed, smiling. But inwardly she was not pleased to see him, and hoped he would not stay for long.

Obviously he had hoped to be invited in, as he had a pair of light shoes with him. Having organised a drink for Kit, Sholto moved away leaving the younger man to give her his present, which was such a charming little carved and painted wooden figure of a Swiss farmer's wife that Armorel felt guilty at wishing him to be gone again.

Clearly everyone else, including Sholto, felt that Kit's arrival must enhance her enjoyment. Even if he had not arrived, she would not have had Sholto as a dancing partner as often as she would have liked—because of his duty to dance with the two other unattached women. As matters turned out it was Diana with whom he danced most often because if Hal was attracted to anyone, it was to Jilly. At least, since their talk on the chair-lift, Armorel was no longer troubled by Sholto's attentiveness to Diana.

In the week between Christmas and New Year, she found herself in the awkward position of being pursued by someone whom she liked too well to rebuff but whose persistent attentions effectively ruined any chance of spending time alone with Sholto, or even with him and other people.

The situation was all the more frustrating because Diana Marshall was spending most of her time with a man she had met on the anchor tow, a very attractive German widower who was staying in the luxury of the Gstaad Palace Hotel. As Jilly and Hal had quite plainly fallen for each other, this meant that Sholto, when not skiing alone on runs fit for experts only, spent most of his time with the Bocage family or with the Hammonds. But for Kit, Armorel could have joined in these group activities. The most maddening thing was that, when she tried tactfully to wriggle out of going about with him, the others, with good intentions, would conspire with him and against her.

'It's so nice for you to have a friend in your own age group,' said Mrs Hammond, on one of these occasions, when Armorel was making excuses not to go out with him. 'The boys are a little too young, and the rest of us are too old for you.'

'I really think I should spend more time with the others, Kit,' said Armorel, on another occasion.

'They don't mind you coming with me. Why should they? Never tell me you'd rather be skating sedately with the oldsters than having a ball with our lot,' he said.

It was on the tip of her tongue to tell him she was not having a ball, and had not grown to like his companions any better than she had when she first met them. The air in their chalet was always dense with cigarette smoke, and she suspected that some of them also smoked pot. They were not keeping the place as clean as it should be, and sometimes they made jokes which she did not fully understand but which instinct told her were off-colour.

She had the uneasy feeling that, when she was not present, Kit used the same crude expletives and laughed at the lewd-sounding jokes. Perhaps it was prudish of her to be embarrassed by the girl who, inside the chalet, always displayed her breasts in skin-tight tee-shirts or see-through blouses. Armorel felt sure that some of Kit's friends, perhaps all of them, thought her a prig, and that was something she had no wish to be. So she went on hiding her distaste for many of their ways, torn between being true to herself and the fear that, because of her background, her ideas were behind the times.

When, on December 30th, she dug in her heels and said she must spend the next night at home, at Sholto's New Year party, Kit tried to make her change her mind.

Eventually he accepted that she was adamant, but later, to her dismay, he asked Sholto if he might join their party.

'Oh, Kit, don't you think it's rude not to see the New Year in with your friends?' she objected.

'They know I would rather be with you,' he answered. 'You don't mind if I muscle in on your celebrations, I hope, sir?'—this to Sholto, to whom his manner was always exaggeratedly respectful as if they were a generation apart in age instead of less than a decade.

Sholto glanced rather thoughtfully at her, and she tried to convey the message that she did not want Kit to come to their New Year party.

But if he received it, he ignored it. 'Not at all, Kit.'

Afterwards, she realised that, short of being discourteous, there was no way in which he could have refused so direct a request.

Thus it was that, at midnight the next night, she found herself clasped in Kit's arms, being kissed with a good deal more fervour than on the several previous occasions when he had attempted some necking and she had fended him off.

When he let her go the first thing she saw, on the other side of the room, was Sholto watching them, his expression at its most sardonic. In the first five minutes of the New Year he kissed all the other women and wished them well, but he did not kiss Armorel, and she felt the omission like a blow.

To her relief, Kit and his party left Gstaad on the second of January, as did the Hammonds and the Bocage family; Ellen Bocage having invited Armorel to spend Easter with them in Paris.

This left only Hal and Diana whose German friend, Gunter, invited them all to dine with him at the hotel on the night of the others' departure.

For Armorel it was, in some ways, the most enjoyable evening of the whole holiday because the two other couples were so intent on each other that Sholto was left with no choice but to concentrate his attention on her.

After dinner Gunter had arranged a sleigh ride, in three separate sleighs.

'You may as well stay here until the end of your holiday. I have to leave in the morning,' said Sholto, as their sleigh, the last of the three to set off, began to slide over the hard-packed snow outside the hotel.

'I daresay you'll find it rather flat without Kit Harper,' he added, tucking the fur rug more snugly round her.

'Actually Kit became a nuisance. One of their party fell out at the last moment, making their number uneven. Otherwise I don't think we should have seen nearly as much of him,' she said, in case Sholto should be under the mistaken impression that she had fallen for Kit.

'You didn't appear to object to his attentions,' he said dryly.

'I didn't want to hurt his feelings.'

'I daresay they're fairly resilient. The ability tactfully to brush off importunate admirers is something you have yet to learn.'

'You didn't help,' she pointed out. 'No one did. Everyone seemed to assume that Kit and I were soul-mates.'

'Not I,' said Sholto. 'Harper didn't impress me as having any distinguishing qualities, and I didn't like the people he was with.'

'I didn't know you knew anything about them.'

'I made it my business to find out. Up to a point you must make your own mistakes about people but, had he tried to embroil you in one of their wilder parties, I should have intervened then. As long as you're under my aegis, I shan't leave you unprotected among the sort of well-heeled layabouts who made up that crowd.'

She received this statement with mixed feelings; part of her resenting his assumption that she couldn't take care of herself, and part of her knowing this was true, and being warmed and pleased by the discovery that he had been taking more notice of her than she had realised. It crossed her mind that, in some people's eyes, being under the aegis of Sholto Ransome was a much more perilous situation than being involved with Kit and his friends.

She said, 'Things seem to be working out rather differently for the others than what you had in mind when you asked them.'

'Yes, and Gunter and Diana seem to be very well suited. I'm less sure about Hal and Jilly. Are you certain you're warm enough?'

'Mm ... beautifully snug, thank you. I feel like a Czarist princess in her troika, except that they had three horses to pull them, I think.'

Armorel fell silent, listening to the jingle of the sleigh bells and the shush of the runners on the snow. All that was needed to make it perfect was for Sholto to hold her hand under the rug or, better still, to put his arm round her.

But he did not touch her and, next day, immediately after breakfast, he left for the Gstaad-Grund heliport where a helicopter was waiting to take him to Geneva. She did not see him again until, while she was staying with the Bocage family at Easter, he spent one night there.

By the end of her final term at the Château, Armorel had decided that as she still had not developed a bent in any particular direction, she would next spend a year on the books of a London agency which supplied temporary office staff. She had been assured that, because she was now an efficient typist and speed-writer, she could, with

her several languages, command a good salary on which
to support herself. And it meant she would not be com-
mitted to a job which might quickly became boring.

Jane had left the Château a term earlier, and her grandmother had pulled strings to secure her a job behind the
scenes at one of the great London auction houses.

'Where she has great hopes either that I shall captivate
a duke coming in to sell off a few Canalettos, or the
millionaire collector who buys them,' said Jane who,
unbeknown to her grandparents, was already more than
half in love with one of her brother's fellow-students.

When it came to finding somewhere to live, Sholto
offered a flat which he owned, suggesting that as Jane was
dissatisfied with her digs, the two girls should share it. At
first Armorel resisted this proposal, feeling the time had
come for her to be fully independent, and that the rent he
suggested was not realistic. But it was difficult to find
anywhere else she liked, and Jane was becoming increasingly restive in her digs, so in the end she capitulated.

The flat was unfurnished, but Sholto reminded her that
she had two chairs and a bookcase in storage, and he
would have them delivered for her. When they arrived she
discovered that he had had them restored for her, but
not to the extent of spoiling them as Jane said was often
the case when auctioned furniture fell into the hands of
some dealers and was done up to look like new. Instead
of the remnants of furnishing fabric put on the chairs by
Miss Newbolt, they now had needlework seats of the kind
they might have had originally.

One Sunday afternoon, while Jane was out with her
medical student, Sholto came to the flat and found
Armorel busy running up, on Mrs Bruce's sewing
machine which she had borrowed for a week, curtains
and bedcovers from stylish, inexpensive cottons by Laura
Ashley and Habitat.

She gave him China tea and brownies she had baked herself. While he was there he said to her, 'By the way, I haven't seen you wearing your locket lately. It should be insured, you know. If you'll give it to me I'll have it valued for you. If you attend to it yourself they'll charge you at least one per cent. My man will do it for nothing.'

Armorel's heart sank. She had hoped he would never notice that she no longer wore the locket because she had not often done so when she had had it. To give herself time to think, she said, 'I've never seen you wearing any jewellery, Sholto.'

'No, I don't care for it on men. But my grandmother left me several antique pieces which are the basis of a collection I've made for investment purposes, and to which I add from time to time when an example of the finest workmanship turns up. Even the best modern jewels can't compare with the best antique pieces. Have you ever seen a *tremblant* flower brooch in which some of the diamonds are set so that they actually quiver at the slightest movement?'

'I haven't. It sounds lovely.'

'Perhaps one of these days I'll take you along to the bank and show you some of the most interesting pieces.'

'Thank you, I should like to see them. It seems rather a shame for such things to have to be kept locked up in a vault, never to be worn again.'

'Some of them will be worn eventually—by my wife.'

Startled, she asked, 'You're getting married?'

'I expect to marry sooner or later.'

'Oh . . . I see. I thought you meant you had someone in mind already.'

She expected him to shake his head, instead of which he did not answer the remark, his silence reviving the curious pain which had pierced her a few seconds earlier.

'Perhaps you have. Anyone I know?' she asked, trying to keep her tone light.

He gave her an enigmatic glance. 'Contain your curiosity, Armorel. You'll be among the first to know when I decide to change my status. Now run along and get your locket, would you?'

'I can't. I—I've lost it,' she told him.

'Lost it? When? In what circumstances?'

'If I knew that, I might have found it again.'

He gave her a long frowning stare which she tried to meet with composure.

At length he said coldly, 'I've always been able to tell when people are trying to bamboozle me. My built-in lie detector tells me that you're being less than truthful. Out with it, Armorel. What really happened to your locket?'

She saw that he meant to grill her until she confessed. 'If you must know, I sold it to pay for something else I wanted.'

'To whom did you sell it?'

'Really, Sholto! Is that any of your business?'

'I think it is. Until you're twenty-one, I've appointed myself as your watch-dog. If some third-rate jeweller has done you down, he'll find he has me to deal with.'

'I didn't go to a third-rate jeweller, and I'm quite sure the price they gave me was a very fair one. The locket wasn't in perfect condition.'

'I should imagine that your knowledge of the value of antique jewellery is on a par with your knowledge of integral calculus—nil,' he said crushingly. 'You'd better tell me the price you got.'

'What a bully you are!' she said rebelliously. But she knew he would have no compunction in browbeating her into revealing the information he wanted and so, reluctantly, she gave it.

It was by no means the end of his cross-examination.

As she might have foreseen, next he became determined to discover why she had needed such a sum in addition to her allowance. Against giving this information she resisted more doggedly, but in the end, greatly exasperated, she said, 'I wanted to buy a present for someone ... to buy it with my own money.'

'A present for whom? For Kit Harper?'

'Perhaps. I'm not going to say. I pity your wife if you mean to harry her like this every time she has some little secret she wants to keep from you.'

A flash of amusement lit his eyes. 'I shall have ways of making her talk which are not applicable in your case.'

'Well, you'll have to stick pins into me before I shall tell,' she said mutinously. 'I'm entitled to *some* private life.'

Her words had a strange effect on him. The smiling look changed to a sudden blaze of black anger from which, instinctively, she cowered. His hands shot out, grabbed her shoulders, and held her a prisoner.

'*You will tell me*,' he said, through clenched teeth.

His rage was both mystifying and terrifying. What had she said to ignite this thunder-clap of ire?

'It . . . it was for you, Sholto,' she stammered. 'Th-the picture I gave you for Christmas.' Her eyes brimmed with sudden hot tears.

'What? Oh, God! For a moment I thought——'

The sentence was never completed. As the tears overflowed down her cheeks, he pulled her against him and hugged her.

'Don't cry, silly child. I'm not going to beat you.'

It was the most intimate moment in their relationship since the day, long ago, when he had kissed her to erase the unpleasantness of the seaman's kiss. She remembered how, ages ago, on a fresh spring morning in his sister's garden in Kent, he had suspected her unhappiness and she had longed to step into his arms and pour out her troubles. Now she was in his arms, her face half hidden against his shoulder, and it felt just as comfortable and secure as she had imagined it would.

'What *did* you think?' she asked huskily, raising her wet face to his.

At first he did not reply, but produced a clean linen handkerchief and dried her cheeks, keeping his other arm round her.

'Tell me, Sholto,' she persisted.

Then she wished she had held her tongue because the second time she asked he put her gently away from him.

'I've lived too long among people whose motives and moral values, my own included, have made me cynical,' he answered. 'As far as I know, no one has ever been moved to part with something of great sentimental value to them in order to buy me a present.'

'Perhaps you have never been as kind to anyone as you have to me.'

'It hasn't been difficult for me to be kind to you, but I think it must have been very difficult for you to part with your only memento of your mother.'

'You looked so enraged. What could you have thought I'd done?'

His expression became oddly sombre. 'You look misleadingly sophisticated, and such false impressions can be dangerous. It crossed my mind that you might have let your feeling run away with you, with a young man who thought you were more worldly wise than you are. That's a situation which, even today, keeps a certain type of clinic in business.'

'Why did it make you so angry to think that might have happened to me? You're not a narrow-minded puritan like my grandfather.'

'Far from it,' was his sardonic comment. 'But that

doesn't mean that I think the lax standards of our day are necessarily an improvement on the too strict standards of his day. I don't think you're the type to take easily to casual love affairs.'

'I know I'm not,' she agreed. 'I want just one great big love affair—the kind which will last all my life. But I expect you think that's silly.'

'No, I think it's rare,' he remarked. 'The only case that I know of is that of my own grandparents, and their marriage was arranged for them by their families. They fell in love later, so my grandmother once told me.'

At this point they were interrupted and, left to herself, she realised she could no longer convince herself that her feelings for Sholto would pass. He was the one love of her life; always had been, and always would be.

A few weeks before Armorel's twenty-first birthday, Sholto rang her up at the office where she was working and asked her to lunch with him at his flat. There he told her that as he did not wish to be seen to be the host at her celebration party, he had arranged for it to be held in the Bocage mansion in Paris.

'Make a list of the English people you want to be there, and I'll arrange for a plane to fly them over and back again. If anyone raises their eyebrows, you can say— with some truth since I am, in effect, your family—that Adrian is a family friend.'

'I don't think there are any people I should like to be there except Jane, and she has already accepted an invitation to spend that weekend with someone special—or rather, with his parents. So I'm hoping she won't remember it will be an occasion for me.'

'In that case, why not take a couple of weeks off and come to Paris when I do, the weekend before? That will give you time to choose a dress at one of the *couture* houses. I want you to be a credit to me, even if not too publicly.'

Armorel arrived for the final fitting for her party dress too early, and while she was waiting and glancing through a copy of the French edition of *Vogue*, someone said in French, 'Don't I know you?'

She looked up to find herself being studied by an elegant vision in white whom she recognised at once.

She jumped to her feet, exclaiming, 'Madame Lamartine! How are you? Yes, we met a long time ago when I was a pupil at the Château de Polignac. You came there one day with Sholto and took me out to lunch. Do you remember?'

'Ah, yes, that's right, I remember now,' the actress said, switching to English. 'But you've changed a great deal since that day. When we met before you had only the promise of being a beauty. Now you are one.'

'Thank you. From someone as beautiful as yourself, that's a great compliment.'

Sidonie sat down on the grey velvet cushioned sofa where Armorel had been waiting for her appointment.

'Alas, my looks now owe more and more to artifice. I have recently had my first face-lift,' she confided, with rather startling candour. 'It would have depressed me except that, after it, I met a charming young man who has fallen in love with me, and who doesn't appear to realise that I am much older than he is. How long it will last between us, who can say? But while it does, it is very enjoyable. Tell me, how is Sholto? It must be six months since I saw him. Is he well?'

'Yes, very well. He's coming to pick me up in half an hour. I'm here for a fitting for the dress for my twenty-first birthday party.'

'I see. Then perhaps I will wait and say hello to him.

You realise, no doubt, that there was a time when he and I were ... very close.'

Armorel nodded. 'I guessed that.'

'It ended by mutual consent, so there is still friendship between us. To meet is not an embarrassment, for him or for me,' said Sidonie. 'That is nice, when a love affair becomes an affectionate friendship. Not that we see each other often, but he still sends me flowers on my birthday, and I know that if I were in trouble I could ask his help and not be refused. I have a small piece of his heart—as have several others. Perhaps one day he will take all those pieces back and give his whole heart to one woman. Do you think?'

'I don't know. I've no idea. It doesn't seem likely,' said Armorel.

At this point she was summoned to her fitting, and Sidonie asked if she might accompany her. The actress sat in silence while the dress was lifted over Armorel's head and smoothed into place on her slender body, but when the fitter began to make minute adjustments to it, she asked, 'And what of your life, my dear? Is there one particular young man, or is your heart free for the present?'

'There's no one special at the moment.'

As usual, Sholto's arrival was punctual to a second. He kissed Sidonie's hand and suggested that they should adjourn to a large hotel and have a drink together.

'I have a better suggestion. Come and see my new apartment. It's not far, and I'm sure the decor would interest Armorel,' said Sidonie. 'It has been designed for me by Alberto Pinto, of whom I expect you have heard?' she added, turning to the English girl.

Armorel nodded. 'I should love to see it, madame. Is there time, Sholto?'

'By all means.'

He had come by taxi, but Sidonie had her car waiting for her. On this occasion she sat in the centre of the seat, with the others on either side of her.

Armorel looked across her at Sholto's strong, starkly-cut profile as he listened to the actress talking about the film she was about to start making. Once or twice he glanced sideways at her, but mostly he looked ahead at the route they were taking. Clearly Sidonie's beauty no longer commanded his attention as it had the last time Armorel had seen them together.

She thought with a pang how terrible it must be to have ignited his passion and then to see the fire burn out, never to be rekindled. Sidonie seemed not to mind the death of their once ardent love affair; but Armorel knew that, in her place, she would find his indifference unbearable. Not that he was ever likely to gaze at her as once he had gazed at Sidonie's lovely face. Long ago, the first time he had seen her after her recovery from her privations in the Pacific, she had thought she had seen the hot flare of lust in his eyes. But that was two years ago, and since then his manner towards her had, in general, been cool and impersonal.

When they arrived at Sidonie's apartment, she suggested that Armorel should wander through it at will while she and Sholto conversed in the living-room.

'Go where you like. Nowhere is private,' she invited.

In her tour of the place, Armorel made mental notes of several unusual touches, notably the way in which, in the kitchen, plain white ceramic tiles had been hung diagonally to form a diaper pattern topped by bands of narrower border tiles.

When she rejoined the others they were sitting opposite each other on the two modern white sofas which flanked the mirror-clad chimney-breast. Sholto rose as Armorel entered. Less than ten minutes later he rose again, to say goodbye.

On an inexplicable impulse Armorel said, 'Perhaps Madame Lamartine would like to come to the party, Sholto.'

'Yes, do come, Sidonie—if you are free on that night.'

He told her the date and she looked it up in her engagement diary, and said she would be delighted to come.

'Are you pleased with your dress?' he asked Armorel, in the taxi.

'Yes, I think it's lovely. I hope you'll like it,' she answered.

'I'm sure I shall,' he answered, rather abstractedly. She had the feeling his thoughts had already shifted to matters of greater interest to him.

On the night of the party, when Armorel walked down the staircase to join the rest of the household before the guests began to arrive, there was only one person's reaction which really mattered to her. Catching sight of her reflection in the mirror at the turn of the stairs, she saw a tall, slender girl in a dress of fluid black and white goergette which clung to her waist and hips before flaring into a swirl of 1920-ish godets with a hand-rolled hem which showed her slim ankles and the dark red glacé kid sandals which exactly matched the bunch of red silk carnations with long green organdie stalks which were pulled through her narrow black belt. A tiny black sequinned bag on a wrist-loop contained lipstick, scent and a handkerchief, and against her lobes and her throat gleamed the lustrous pearls she had found in a box on her dressing-table when she went up to dress.

Because they were obviously real pearls, she had meant only to try them on, and then to tell Sholto she could not accept such a costly present. But once the single theatre-length strand was clasped round her neck, and the platinum hooks of the ear-drops were fixed in her ears, she found it impossible to resist wearing them—just for tonight.

The others were sitting and standing in a group by the two long sofas, arranged *à l'anglaise* on either side of the fireplace, when she entered the salon.

'Armorel, my dear!'

Ellen Bocage's exclamation made them all fall silent, turning to stare at the figure poised hesitantly on the threshold of the tall double doors.

Armorel knew without looking where Sholto was standing. But her gaze travelled round all the others before coming to rest on his face.

He strolled towards her, his cool eyes scrutinising every detail of her appearance. He himself was wearing that most becoming of all masculine apparel, a lightweight tropical dinner jacket over a shirt of finely pin-tucked white lawn with a narrow silk bow tie and trousers of black silk worsted with a fine line of black silk braid down the outside seam. Not for Sholto the flamboyance of the frilled shirts and velvet bows affected by television personalities. Not only could he afford the most superb cloth, the finest bespoke tailoring, but his athletic physique needed nothing to set it off beyond the discreet perfection which he wore with such careless ease.

As she looked admiringly at him, she was startled to see in his eyes the sudden bright gleam of desire she remembered from two years before. His glance lingered on her hips, on the low décolletage of her dress where his string of pearls lay between her half-exposed breasts, and finally on her mouth, painted deep red to match her shoes and the bunch of flowers at her waist.

He said nothing, but took her hand and brushed her knuckles with his lips, his grey eyes conveying a message which brought a warm wash of colour into her cheeks.

'Th-thank you for these,' she stammered, touching the pearls.

'It isn't often that pearls have such a perfect setting.'

Unseen by the others behind him, he studied the curves of her bosom with a look as intimate and unnerving as a physical caress.

She was blushing and her heart was thumping as, still holding her hand, he turned and led her among the others. If her confusion was noticeable, probably they attributed it to nervous excitement, although as the evening went on Sholto made no secret of his changed attitude to her.

She remembered him saying to her, on the day they had gone back to her island and he had kissed her, 'Don't worry: I have no intention of repeating it—or at least not until you are very much older and wiser.'

Now, it seemed, that time had come and before the party had been in progress for an hour, she had no doubt that when it was over he would kiss her again, and perhaps not as lightly as the first time.

He left it to others to partner her in the lively dances, claiming her for himself only when the music was sweet and slow and he could hold her against him, his arm tightening round her if she attempted to draw away. After a few vain attempts to keep a space between their bodies, she gave in and submitted to being pressed to his tall strong frame.

It had not been from distaste that she had sought at first to avoid the close contact; but rather from fear that she might not be able to hide from him, or from anyone watching them, some sign of the tremors she felt at being locked in his powerful right arm, her softness crushed to his hardness from chest to hip and hip to knee, so that at every turn she felt his long muscular thighs against her legs.

'I like your scent. What is it?' he asked.

'*Mystère* by Rochas.'

'Which of your admirers sees you as a woman of mystery?'

'None of them. It was a present from Jane. Speaking of presents, I—I don't think you should have given me such a valuable birthday present, Sholto. Your pearls are gorgeous, but——'

'But you're beginning to wonder if they may have strings attached to them, is that it?' he finished for her.

She flashed a swift upward glance at the lean, sun-tanned face above hers, and found him watching her with a quizzical glint in his eyes and a slight smile twisting his mouth.

'No—no, of course not,' she began.

'But you're right—there are strings,' he said.

Her heart gave a violent lurch which she felt sure he must have felt.

'W-what do you mean?'

'As you correctly surmise, no man gives jewels to a woman to whom he's not related without some designs upon her, of one sort or another. But this is hardly the time or the place to discuss it, do you think? Later perhaps, or tomorrow as it seems more than likely your party will go on till dawn.'

The music stopped and he released his hold of her body but not of her hand. With his right hand he touched one of the pearl eardrops and then, for an instant or two, his first and second fingertips explored the warm place behind her ear. It was so brief a caress that probably no one else noticed it, but its effect on Armorel was almost as disturbing as if he had touched her where the centre pearl of the necklace lay close to her low-cut neckline. She had never thought of the backs of her ears as being a private part of her anatomy, or the skin there as being more than ordinarily sensitive to amorous touches. But when Sholto touched her there she found it almost painfully exciting. She dared not let her mind dwell on the effect he would have if they were alone and he chose to exert all his expert knowledge of how to make women abandon their inhibitions. She knew she would be helpless to resist him.

It was time to go to the supper room where Ellen Bocage had organised a lavish cold table with champagne to drink and a dozen different delicacies to eat. There, Sholto and Armorel became separated, giving her a much-needed respite from the magnetism of his personality, and time to get used to the idea that, now that she was fully and indisputably of age in everyone's eyes including those of people who felt that an eighteen-year-old was not completely mature, she was about to become the next on the list of his girl-friends.

It was a wonder to her that, with such a momentous change in her life looming over her, she was able to swallow a crumb; but somehow she managed to put on a show of normality and even to carry on lighthearted conversations with the people around her. No one seemed to detect that she was not really enjoying the lobster roulade and the champagne.

She knew that if Sholto had made up his mind to take her to his bed, there was only one way to frustrate him, and that was to run away. It would mean breaking the thread of her life in London, and leaving the flat and the friends she had made. She would have to make a fresh start somewhere else, somewhere where he could not find her. The alternative was to stay and share his life for as long as she pleased him. And really why not? a voice seemed to murmur—the voice of the sensuous side of her nature, normally dormant but now aroused as never before, and hungry for fulfilment.

To this, the intellectual side of her could return a number of arguments, of which the foremost was that it would be degrading, not only to her but to her sex as a whole, to allow him to make her his plaything; a toy to be enjoyed and discarded as soon as he tired of her.

That she was capable of exciting his interest at all affirmed what she knew from her mirror: that she had been lucky enough to inherit more than ordinary good looks. But she was not so vain as to suppose that she had what a woman as alluring as Sidonie Lamartine had lacked—the power to keep Sholto attracted to her for life.

Any sexual relationship she entered with him was, she knew, inevitably doomed to impermanence. Perhaps it was the nature of any man who could have all the women he wanted never to be satisfied with one. Why, indeed, should he be, when always there would be some new beauty ready to fall like a ripe fruit into his hand?

In the case of Sidonie, clearly the beautiful actress was the female equivalent of a womaniser. But Armorel knew that it was not in her own nature to engage in love lightly. For her, love must always be deep and consuming, leaving scars—if it ended unhappily—which would never be healed. Was the heaven of being Sholto's love for a few weeks or months worth the hell of despair which must follow?

I would sell my soul if it would make him love me for life, but I won't sacrifice my self-respect for a short time of flawed happiness, she thought as she ate, without tasting it, a dish of Bavarian cream brought to her by the man who was sitting beside her, trying to charm her.

Sidonie arrived very late, looking ravishing in black crêpe-de-chine with a wide belt of emerald sequins, and accompanied by her latest lover whom Armorel judged to be in the same boat as herself—genuinely in love with someone for whom love was merely a pastime.

Sidonie had brought her, as a present, a small enamelled oval box. On the lid was written 'Happiness is the thing that makes you feel that *now* is the best time of the year'.

'I love little boxes,' the actress explained, 'and when I see one which pleases me, I always buy two—one to keep, and one to give as a present. This box, and my box like it, I found in a shop in London called Halcyon Days. Isn't that a charming name? Oh, my dear, what wonderful pearls! I needn't ask who gave you those. Where is Sholto? I haven't seen him yet.'

'Here,' said a voice behind them, and Sidonie swung round to smile and give him her hand.

Watching the two men shake hands as Sidonie introduced her new lover to him, Armorel realised they were a good deal alike in their air of abundant energy and virility. But already she had the impression that Sidonie's companion was subservient to the actress except, presumably, when they were actually in bed together. He lacked Sholto's careless assurance and look of authority. Although Luigi was the more handsome, it did not make him the more attractive of the two. There was something slightly sulky about his mouth, and his lips were too full. She much preferred Sholto's firm mouth with its full lower lip balanced by a more narrowly cut upper one; the mouth of a man of strong passions but also of strong self-discipline whose emotions would always be held in check except when he chose to unleash them.

She became aware suddenly that Sidonie had made some remark to her which she had not heard because she had been in a trance, her gaze fixed on Sholto's mouth, her mind full of indecision about whether she could bring herself to consent to the proposition he was planning to put to her.

'I'm so sorry—what did you say?'

Sidonie repeated the remark, and Armorel saw in her eyes that the Frenchwoman guessed she had fallen in love with Sholto. She had a crazy impulse to invent a reason to be private with her and ask Sidonie's advice. Instead she showed Sholto the box and, having admired it, he said, 'Shall I put it in my pocket for you?'

'Thank you.' She watched him slip it away in the inside pocket of his dinner jacket, and then he asked Sidonie to dance, and Luigi asked her.

By one o'clock in the morning, in spite of her afternoon rest, she was weary and longing for seclusion. This was not the right mood to be in at a party given in her honour, and in the hope that a short respite from it might refresh her, she made her escape into the garden. There were a number of people strolling about the paved walks under the fairylit trees, but she managed to avoid meeting any of them and to gain the sanctuary of an arbour cut into a high, thick hedge and furnished with a wooden seat.

Seen through the thicket of leaves behind it, the lights of the house were merely a glow in the darkness, and the music reached her only faintly. She looked up at the starlit sky, and felt a sudden deep longing for the different stars of her childhood and untroubled girlhood. Becoming a woman seemed to be fraught with problems.

It was strange that Sholto's intentions towards her should have changed. She had felt sure he had been sincere the day he had found out why she had sold her locket; the day he had told her she was not made to take love lightly—as lightly as he did.

The murmur of approaching voices distracted her from her unhappy reverie. Soon after she recognised the feminine one as Sidonie's distinctively low-pitched drawl. She was not speaking French, so perhaps she and Luigi spoke English together.

But that it was not Luigi to whom she was speaking became clear a few moments later when, apparently coming to a standstill a yard from where Armorel was seated she said, 'Tell me, Sholto, what are your plans with regard to your charming young protégée? The first time I saw her, and even a few days ago when we met again, you seemed not to notice her beauty. But tonight I have seen in your eyes that predatory look with which a man of your type watches a woman who attracts him.'

'Now that she is of age, and has gained some experience of the world in the two years since I first found her, I intend to marry her, Sidonie,' was Sholto's shattering reply.

CHAPTER FIVE

'You have fallen in love with her?' the actress asked.

On the other side of the yew hedge, Armorel held the breath she had drawn in while he was speaking.

'In my observation, love is a weak basis for marriage,' she heard him reply. 'I believe I once told you the circumstances in which Armorel became my protégée.'

'Yes—yes, you did.'

'Only a girl of exceptional courage and stamina could have survived that ordeal. I want that courage, that indomitable grit, in my children. Also, as you say, she is beautiful. But even if she were not, her other qualities would be sufficient for me. Beauty, essential in a mistress, is of less account in a wife,' he said dryly. 'I want my marriage to be permanent. There will be no divorce for us.'

'You are very sure she will have you, my friend.'

'Why should she not? I can give her everything a woman wants. Several youngsters have been in love with her, but none of them seems to have aroused more than a casual affection in her.'

'Has it occurred to you that she may be in love with you? It would not be surprising. You're an attractive devil, and she owes you her life and everything she has.'

'If she is, so much the better,' was his careless answer.

'Ah, there your knowledge of feminine psychology is at fault. If she loves you, she will want to be loved in return,' said the actress. 'For me, the most important thing in life is my work. But for the majority of women it is a man who takes the first place, and for whom, if necessary, they will sacrifice everything else—their careers, their comforts, even their peace of mind.'

To these observations Sholto made no response and, after a pause, his companion continued, 'You said just now that beauty, essential in a mistress, was less important in a wife; and you said also that you could give her everything a woman wants. But while you have all the qualities which make a satisfactory lover—you are very attractive, and also very rich, and generous—perhaps you are not so well equipped to be a husband. From a husband one requires devotion, tenderness as well as passion, friendship as well as sex. Can you give her those things, *mon chéri*?'

'You have problems enough of your own without concerning yourself with my affairs, Sidonie,' was his somewhat curt rejoinder. 'Come, let's go back into the house.'

Armorel heard the Frenchwoman's soft trill of laughter. 'Now I have annoyed you. How naughty of me! But it's no use scowling at me, darling——' The rest of her words became inaudible as they moved out of Armorel's earshot.

For some time she remained where she was, still scarcely able to believe she had actually heard Sholto declare his intention to marry her. Did he mean to ask her tonight? And if he did, what should she say? Say Yes! *Yes!* her eager heart clamoured. To be Mrs Sholto Ransome, could life offer greater fulfilment? And yet, if he did not love her . . .

She returned to the dance, torn between anticipation and apprehension. As soon as she reappeared, a young man claimed her as his partner and, for the rest of the night, she danced every dance, but not again with the one man for whose arms she longed.

At four o'clock in the morning Armorel took off her

dress and hung it carefully away on a padded, satin-covered hanger. Under it, she was wearing nothing but a transparent white body stocking fitted with ribbon suspenders to support pale sheer Dior nylons. Having taken these off but still wearing the shimmery body stocking, she went into the bathroom to take off her make-up and clean her teeth.

When she returned to the bedroom she was startled to see Sholto standing by her dressing-table. At first he had his back to her, but her startled expression made him swing round to face her.

'I did knock,' he said, 'but, there being no answer, I assumed you were having a shower, and came in to leave the box which Sidonie gave you.'

'Oh ... I see. Thank you.'

She hesitated, conscious that she might as well be naked and uncertain whether to retreat into the bathroom, or to dart to the bed where her robe lay.

His gaze raked her slender form and she flushed as his grey eyes lingered on the parts of her normally concealed from him.

'If you're not too tired, I thought we might have a talk. Do you want to finish undressing?' With the glimmer of a smile, he turned his back on her once more.

Armorel moved to the bed. Quickly she peeled off the body stocking and reached for her nightdress. It was then, momentarily nude, that she realised Sholto was watching her in the triple mirrors of the dressing-table which showed him not one but three reflections of her.

Quivering, she snatched up her nightgown and pulled it on and, over it, the matching robe.

'You can turn round. I'm decent now,' she said, in an unsteady voice.

He turned and came slowly towards her, his long lean

fingers at work to undo his bow tie and then to unbutton his collar.

'You enjoyed your party, I hope?'

'Yes, I did, thank you.' She felt the inadequacy of the
words, but was, for the moment, incapable of a more
graceful reply.

The strong brown column of his throat now exposed by
the unfastened shirt sent a little pang of excitement
through her.

'Are you annoyed because I've seen you naked?' he
asked. 'You shouldn't be. A girl with a beautiful body
has no need for any false modesty.'

'Am I beautiful, Sholto?' The words came out in a
whisper.

He was close to her now, his grey eyes curiously
brilliant. 'So much so that, even at this hour of the
morning, I'm tempted to stay with you,' he told her.
'Would you like that?'

Her lashes flickered uncertainly. What did he expect
her to say? Perhaps, if he meant to marry her, he
wanted her to refuse him, to be different from all the
others who had succumbed to him so easily. And yet
the truth was that she wanted desperately to pierce the
mystery of what women really experienced in the arms
of their lovers: not with any man, only with him.

The word 'Yes' trembled on her lips, but was never
uttered because, before she could say it, he had stuffed
his tie into his pocket and taken her neck in both hands.

'All those young men you've known—Harper, Bruce
and the others—has none of them ever made you want
more than a few goodnight kisses?' As he spoke, his
fingers caressed the back of her neck while his thumbs
moved softly under her chin.

She shook her head slightly. 'No, I was never in love
with them.'

His piercing eyes narrowed, mocking her. 'And you think without love there could be no pleasure in making love?'

Again she made a negative movement of her head.

'It doesn't say much for their prowess as lovers. Close your eyes for a moment.'

She obeyed, wondering if he meant to kiss her, longing for it and yet dreading it because she knew that, if he did, she would never be able to think straight, and she wanted to make up her mind without being influenced by her senses.

He did not kiss her; but, very quickly, she discovered that by closing her eyes he had made her doubly aware of the movements of his fingers on her neck. Knowing how strongly his bronzed hands could grip, she was amazed at their gentleness now.

As if he could read her thoughts, he said softly, 'How little you know. The pleasures of the flesh are not dependent upon a state of mind. You could think yourself in love with someone and, if he were an unskilful lover, you might never experience great heights of enjoyment in bed with him. But a man who understood women could make you want him as much as, when you were adrift in the Pacific, you craved for something to eat.'

Her eyes flew open. She put her hands up to his wrists and almost wrenched them away from her.

'A man like yourself, in other words,' she said, in a tight voice. 'Has no woman ever been ... indifferent to you, Sholto?'

'None that I wanted,' he answered.

'Oh!' she exclaimed indignantly. 'Then I think it's high time someone was. It can't be good for anyone's character always to get whatever or whomever they want.'

'Probably not,' he agreed, on a note of amusement.

'Are you going to be the first one to give me that salutory set-down?'

She had moved a short distance away and half-turned her back to him, her white robe of double chiffon clutched around her in an unconscious gesture of self-protection.

Now, turning to face him again, she saw in his eyes the certainty that she was his for the taking. Had she not overheard his conversation with Sidonie pride, if nothing else, would have made her say, 'Yes, I am.' As it was, she ignored the fact that, earlier, he had said he was tempted to stay with her and asked her if she would like it, and said, 'You haven't asked me for anything.'

'If you were a woman in experience as well as years, I shouldn't ask—I should take,' he said. 'But an untried virgin needs rather more gentle handling and, as it's now almost morning, I think perhaps it might be better to celebrate that graduation with another party tonight— *à deux* this time.'

Instead of being relieved, she was conscious of disappointment—and she felt sure he knew it.

'Rest now, and have lunch in bed,' said Sholto. 'I'll see you again in about seven hours. Until then——' With a casually blown kiss, he was gone, leaving her to suspect that he had never really meant to share her bed tonight—or rather this morning—but that he did mean to do so before another night was over.

It was twenty minutes past noon when she woke up, having fallen asleep much more quickly than she had expected, considering the mental and emotional turmoil in which Sholto had left her.

Shortly before one o'clock, the door opened and one of the maids looked in. Seeing that Armorel was awake, she explained that her orders were not to disturb mademoiselle if she were sleeping, but, if she had woken, to bring her a light lunch.

On the lunch tray, when it arrived, there was an envelope with *Armorel* written on it in a bold black hand. The message inside it was brief. She was to meet him at a fashionable café at four. She knew the café he mentioned, having passed it often and sometimes sat in the pavement section, never dreaming it might be the setting for a proposal of marriage. It struck her as profoundly ironic that, having received several previous proposals and refused them because she had not been in love with the men concerned, she should now be contemplating refusing a man whom she did love because he did not love her.

Yet there must be literally hundreds of girls in the world who don't even know him but who would jump at the chance to be his wife because he is attractive and rich. That would be enough for them. Why isn't it enough for me? she wondered, as she ate the avocado and cottage cheese salad, and sipped the chilled white wine, which presumably Sholto had ordered for her.

After lunch she ran a bath and lay in it for fifteen minutes. Then, wrapped in a long towelling robe, she returned to the bedroom to make up her face. She had put on her eyes and was about to outline her lips when there was a light tap at the door.

Expecting to see Ellen, she called, 'Come in,' and was startled when Sholto entered.

'I thought we were meeting at four?' she said.

'Unfortunately something has come up. I have to fly over to London, but before that I have to talk to you.'

The dressing bench was a wide one with room for two people on it. He gestured for her to move up, and sat down with his back to the dressing-table so that he faced one way and she the other, as if on a Victorian love-seat except that there was no barrier of upholstery between them.

'Last night it amused me to tease you a little, but in fact I want you to marry me. Will you let me go on taking care of you, Armorel?'

Although she had known that he meant to offer her marriage, she had not expected to be moved by the way he expressed it; but she was. She was very much moved.

'Why, Sholto? Why?' she asked faintly.

'Because you are beautiful—and brave. Because you are the first woman with whom I have felt the urge to have children,' he told her. 'Because you have all the qualities which I admire in your sex, and none of the faults which irritate me.'

'Are you saying that you love me?'

'I'm being more exact than that. I'm saying that I like your mind and desire your body, and that I have every confidence we can live together in harmony, and raise strong, intelligent children.'

She searched his face for some hint that, deep down, his feelings might be more impassioned than his words. But there was nothing in his expression to give her a flicker of hope that one day she might make him love her as fiercely as she longed to be loved. His grey eyes were calm; his whole manner that of a man propounding a sound business merger rather than a marriage.

She licked her dry lips and swallowed. 'If ... if I accepted your offer, would you continue to have other women?'

'No, I should not,' he said levelly. 'I don't deny that my past has not been ascetic. Why should it have been? It would be extremely unnatural if an unmarried man of my age had not had a number of mistresses. But whatever the scandal rags may have implied at times, my sexual appetite is not in any way abnormal. My wife, as long as she was warm and responsive, would have no cause to be jealous.'

Armorel stared at the sable lip brush which was still in her hand. 'I'm sorry, Sholto. I'm grateful for all your care of me. I can never return your generosity, and I'll always feel ... kindly towards you. But I want to marry for love, not for the down-to-earth reasons which you have set out.'

'Then I shall have to make you love me, shan't I?' he said lightly.

'You can't *make* anyone love you. It ... it's a spontaneous emotion.'

'Are you sure of that?'

As she looked up and met his eyes, he reached out and opened her robe so that he could put his hand on her heart, his lean fingers pressing the soft upper curve of her breast.

'If you feel nothing for me, why does your heart beat so fast?'

'I—I don't know,' she said, her voice husky because her throat was constricted by an almost unbearable tension.

His grey eyes mocked her confusion. 'I think you do know, my girl.'

'W-what do you mean?'

His hand slid further under the towelling in a contact which seemed to burn her bare skin, still moist from her bath. 'You may not love me, in your definition of the term, but I think you would very much like me to teach you to make love.'

'No, please ... you mustn't ... I don't ...' she began, clutching at his strong wrist as his stroking hand threatened completely to wreck her ability to think sensibly.

'Why not?—If I want to teach you, and you want to be taught?' he asked.

'But I don't ... I don't,' she protested.

'Don't you—if you are honest?' He removed his hand from her breast, but only to slide that arm round her while his other hand tilted her chin, forcing her to meet the penetrating look he bent upon her.

Under that searching regard, she found it impossible to prevaricate. 'P-perhaps ... I'm not sure,' she whispered.

'You will be,' he promised her, with a gleam of amusement. 'A month from now you'll be sure, and we'll announce our engagement. And a month after that we'll be married. Meanwhile—reluctantly—I must leave you.'

She saw that he meant to kiss her, and instinctively she closed her eyes a moment before the hard, sensual mouth came down on hers. But his kiss was neither long nor passionate, and in spite of their sometimes ruthless lines, his lips were unexpectedly soft and warm. Even so their touch sent a frisson of wild excitement coursing through her already taut nerves.

He let her go, his eyes mocking. 'That was merely a foretaste. When I come back tomorrow, we'll go a stage further,' he added as he rose from the bench. 'Goodbye, Armorel.'

'Goodbye,' she breathed unsteadily, watching him stride to the door without glancing back as he opened it.

An instant later she was alone again, with her heart pounding even more violently, and her mind in a whirl of confusion.

After what he had said to her, and done to her, it was impossible to concentrate on her make-up. She closed her eyes, remembered his hand on her body and his lips moving softly on hers, and she knew it was true—she

did want him to make love to her. She felt sure that,
with Sholto, even her initiation would be a blissful experience; not the disappointing anticlimax which some
girls seemed to suffer at the hands of inexperienced or
clumsy lovers.

She wondered what he had meant by saying that
tomorrow they would go a stage further, and she wished
she had had the courage to slide her arms round his neck
and encourage him to stay a little longer and teach her
a little more immediately.

The brief kiss had left her curiously unsatisfied, as
perhaps he had meant that it should. What would it be
like if he lost control of himself? The thought of it
frightened and thrilled her. He had stirred something
primitive in her; and she sensed that he, too, had a
primitive side to his nature which it would not do to
arouse—or only if she were prepared to take the violent
consequences.

Yet even while her body trembled with anticipatory
pleasure, her mind rebelled against the careless assurance
of his plans for their future. He did not love her; nor did
he require her to love him. Apparently he found her
physically desirable, and saw certain qualities in her
which he thought might come out in his children. All
too clearly she saw that, in his eyes, the fundamental
role of a wife was not that of a friend and partner but
of a bed-mate and brood-mare. Were it not for his
desire for children—sons, no doubt, in preference to
daughters—probably he would never marry.

For a long time she sat there, her mind and her body
at war; her body clamouring for the sensuous delights
she knew he could give her, *par excellence*; and her mind
insisting that passion alone was not enough.

It did not take him a month to make her agree to marry

him. He accomplished it in a fortnight. From the moment he returned from London, he gave all his time to her. Often, during those two weeks she remembered Jane quoting her mother as saying, of men, 'It's nice if they're good-looking, too, but it really doesn't matter a jot as long as they're sweet to you and make you laugh.'

No one could have been sweeter to her than Sholto. Every morning on her breakfast tray there would be a surprise for her, sometimes expensive, sometimes not, but always charming. Very often, even if they had been out late the night before, there would be a note from him saying that he would be downstairs within the hour to take her into the country.

They spent a good deal of time in the museums of Paris, mostly in the galleries devoted to paintings and the applied arts. In one of his more serious moods, Sholto told her that for him a museum took the place of a church in the life of a religious person. An hour spent studying the finest artefacts of their own or other civilisations refreshed him when he was depressed by the political scene and reports from the parts of the world still given over to barbarism.

But sometimes, when they were standing on either side of a showcase containing some rare and beautiful object, she would find him looking not at it but at her and, when their eyes met, he would hold her gaze with a curiously hypnotic force so that it was an effort to smile and turn away to look at something else, trying not to let him guess that her heart was beating an excited tattoo.

Often they would sit in pavement cafés where either he would make her laugh with dry comments about the passers-by or absurd jokes, or he would shift his chair in order to study her with the same close attention he gave to a piece of rare porcelain or the pattern on an ancient bronze dish. Armorel found these caressing scrutinies difficult to bear with equanimity and, try as she would to control it, a flush would creep into her cheeks when his eyes conveyed, unmistakably, the message that much as he liked the way she was dressed, he would prefer to see her undressed.

Having made her blush, he would smile and reach across the table for her hand which he would kiss, sometimes on the knuckles and sometimes, more disturbingly, in the palm.

One day, when he was looking at her in this way, to distract him she said, 'Has it ever occurred to you, Sholto, that I may have very bad blood in me, on my father's side? Aunt Rose always spoke of him as being a most disreputable type.' Thinking of what he had told Sidonie, she added, 'I'm sure you wouldn't wish your children to have a crook—which he might be now— for a grandfather.'

'Not if he played a leading role in your life,' he agreed. 'But he doesn't—never has. You don't even think about him often, do you?'

'Not often. One can't help being slightly curious about one's parents if one has never known them. What does worry me slightly sometimes is the possibility of ... well, no, not blackmail, but of excessive cadging. If he found out that I was married to someone very rich, I mean.'

'You can forget that forthwith. If your father ever did show up, which seems to me highly improbable, I should know how to deal with him if he attempted anything of that nature.'

'But if he threatened to expose the circumstances of my birth, wouldn't that be an embarrassment to you?'

'In this day and age? My dear girl, what does it matter?—— To you, or to me, or to anyone? Am I to take it that you're beginning to accept that our future lies together?'

'I don't know ... I still don't know.'

On secluded walks in the country, and before they parted at night after an evening together, he would go somewhat further than looking desirously at her, or pressing his lips into her palm. But he never went further, or as far, as the various men she had dated since working in London.

Their approaches had varied from the tentative to the irritating assumption that taking her out to dinner entitled them to spend the night with her. Sholto was never tentative, but neither did he advance beyond what broadminded parents, if she had had any, would have considered allowable on the part of a man who had already proposed marriage to her.

Sometimes Armorel found herself wishing he would go further, a lot further. There were moments when she longed to be swept off her feet by his ardour; to be flung on the grass in some isolated forest glade and made love to with her consent being taken for granted.

One night, after they had dined out with Adrian and Ellen, and returned to the house for several nightcaps and an hour's conversation, her host and hostess went to bed and left them alone in one of the smaller, less formal salons in the house.

They had been on their own for about five minutes after the others had said goodnight, when Sholto surprised her by leaving the chair where he was sitting and crossing the room to lock the tall double doors. As he returned from the doorway, he took off his tie and unfastened the collar of his shirt as he had in the early hours of the day after her twenty-first birthday party.

She was sitting on a giltwood bergère upholstered with blue moiré silk. When he held out his hand to her, she took it and let him pull her up and—as she thought—into his arms. Instead he swung her off her feet and carried her across to a long four-seater, feather-cushioned sofa, one of several pieces of comfortable American furniture which Ellen had introduced into the elegant, very French decoration of the house.

Having lowered her on to the sofa, he sat on its edge, close beside her, and looked at her for a few moments with a smiling glint in his eyes, and something else, too; a look which reminded her of the first time he had set eyes on her when she had recovered her figure after becoming so emaciated. She had never forgotten that look, or the way he had made her feel like a captive slave girl being appraised by a buyer. Now she felt the same way, only this time she had the momentary illusion that she had become his possession and he was about to put her to the use for which he had bought her.

As he swooped to kiss her, her heart lurched with nervous excitement, and then she was locked in his arms, being kissed with a fierce, devouring passion which felt like being caught by a wave and tossed helplessly hither and thither by a force so strong and relentless that all one could do was submit.

And yet before it was over, that first long, searching, hungry kiss, there was more than submission in her response. Her lips moved, her body arched, her arms slid round him and clung. This was what, deep down, she had wanted: to be overpowered, coerced, mastered.

It was not all fierceness and conquest, that interlude on the sofa. At times he was very gentle with her, his lips light and warm on her throat, the touch of his fingertips feather-soft. She was wearing a Mary Farrin dress, a pale grey cobwebby garment knitted from a yarn as fine as the thread in a Shetland shawl, and made in a style reminiscent of the 1930s with a peplum from waist to hip, a draped cowl neck and cape sleeves. The skirt had a thin silk lining, and under the top she was wearing the lightest possible seamless bra. Sholto did not attempt to undress her, as she expected he would, but his hands searched her yielding body through the gossamer fabric until she was driven half-delirious by the practised skill of his kisses, and the sensuous movements of his hands. She heard herself making small incoherent murmurs of pleasure, but she couldn't help it. She began to ache with the longing for him to touch her bare flesh, not just on her neck and arms but everywhere.

It was then, while she was discovering the hitherto unrealised voluptuousness of her own nature, that he said, his mouth close to her ear, 'Can you tell me now you don't love me?'

She opened her eyes, and answered, without hesitation, 'Oh, yes, darling—yes, I adore you.'

He gave her one more burning kiss which forced from her a stifled groan of delight. Then he sat up, and while she lay lax on the cushions, dazedly watching his lean dark face in the soft light from one large table lamp, he took from his pocket a ring-box.

'May I put this on now?'

'This' was the flashing green fire of a huge square emerald framed with diamonds.

'Sholto!' she gasped.

He slipped it on to her finger, and kissed her hand. 'I don't think the others will be in bed yet. I told them I hoped they would be able to congratulate me before the night was out, and I know there's some champagne on ice. Shall I call them down to share it with us?'

Without waiting for her answer, he rose to unlock the door and to use the internal telephone.

'Oh, give me a minute to collect myself,' she exclaimed. 'My hair . . . what must I look like?'

She jumped up and rushed to a mirror where, as well as her own reflection, she saw him watching her and smiling.

'Like Eve after her first proper bite at the apple,' he told her. Then, into the telephone, he said, 'Ellen? I'm happy to say that Armorel has agreed to marry me. Will you join us for a little celebration?'

She had re-painted her mouth, from which he had kissed all the lipstick and left slightly swollen and tender, and was busy with her hair when he came up behind her. As she stood with both arms raised, one hand combing, the other patting, he put his arms round her and ran both hands over her body from her collarbones to her hipbones.

She shuddered. 'Oh, please . . . don't Sholto. They may come in at any moment.'

'Not yet.' With slow deliberation his hands retraced their route upwards and, unable to meet the rather mocking gleam of understanding in the grey eyes looking over her head, she closed her eyes.

'I don't think you knew you could feel like this, did you?' he said.

'No,' she said breathlessly. 'No, I didn't. Oh!'—this last exclamation as he bent and gently bit the nape of her neck, sending yet another violent tremor through her.

Then, abruptly, he let her go, and walked away across the room so that when the door opened to admit Ellen, followed by her husband, they were standing several yards apart and only Armorel's flushed cheeks gave some clue as to how closely and intimately he had been holding her to him minutes before.

They had been engaged for some days before it dawned upon her that Sholto's behaviour towards her, unremittingly amorous during the preceding fortnight, had undergone a sudden and inexplicable change. Since the night of their engagement not once had he said or done anything to make her heart begin to race as it had so frequently done during the two weeks of his relentless, overpowering courtship. Then, he had seized every moment of privacy to touch her. But now that they were officially engaged, he had become as circumspect as if they had an invisible chaperone with them at all times. She could not understand it.

During their pre-engagement period, whenever they had gone out at night their transport had been a large limousine with a chauffeur or, sometimes a taxi. In the limousine Sholto had kissed her. Even in the taxis—not as private as those in London— he had always put his arm round her and murmured ardent remarks in her ear. Since their engagement, however, he had taken to driving her himself and, perversely, instead of being relieved that he had to keep his eyes on the road and his hands on the wheel, she began to feel rather piqued.

One night, after going to the theatre with him, she said, 'Do you realise it's five days since you kissed me, except on the cheek?'

He shot a swift sideways glance at her. 'Where would you like me to kiss you?'

'Don't tease, Sholto. Considering how ... pressing you were until very recently, it's a rather noticeable change, that's all. You aren't having second thoughts, are you?'

'On the contrary, I'm beginning to feel that a month-long engagement is three weeks too long.'

'One would never think it! Before we became engaged you made love to me, in one way or another, practically all the time. Since then you don't even hold my hand at the theatre.'

'I thought you would guess the reason for my restraint now. One forgets how innocent you are.'

'What do you mean?'

'For you the words "making love" means holding hands, kissing, touching—within certain limits. For me there are no such limits; and there've been several occasions when I've been tempted to show you what I mean by those two words. I haven't done so because I felt you would prefer to wait until our wedding night. Was I wrong about that?'

'No .... you were right. I would rather wait,' she admitted. 'It's old-fashioned of me, I know, but some-how——' She hesitated, finding it difficult to put her feelings into words.

'Your innocence in a corrupt world is part of your charm for me, Armorel,' he said, before she could express herself. 'I don't mind waiting a little longer, if that's what you prefer. But don't make the mistake of thinking I'm not impatient. It wouldn't take much to break down my good intentions.'

The car slid to a halt at traffic lights, and he took his right hand off the gear lever and put it on her left knee, pushing back her skirt the length of her thigh, making her give the little indrawn gasp of disconcertion which had been her frequent reaction in the time before their engagement.

'Which is why,' he went on, 'it's wiser for me not to touch you, except in circumstances which make it impossible for me to go too far.'

In the final few seconds before the traffic lights changed his fingers tightened on her leg, and she saw in his eyes a flare of desire which would have convinced her if what he had said had not done so.

Then the traffic began to move forward, and Sholto drove on, leaving her to straighten her disarranged skirt and wait for her sensitised nerves to recover from his possessive touch.

In the courtyard of the Bocage house, he shut off the engine, and she expected him to get out and walk round to open her door for her.

Instead, he turned to her, and said, 'One kiss—not on the cheek!'

It was the kind of kiss which, until the night he had put the ring on her finger, he had always led up to with other preparatory kisses. This time as on their engagement night there were no gentler preliminaries. His warm mouth closed over hers and forced from her a response which left her breathless and trembling.

'You see what I mean?' he said huskily. 'Out you get. I'll see you tomorrow.'

Reaching across her, he opened the nearside door and gave her a gentle push. She had scarcely pushed the door shut before the car was in motion, circling the courtyard in a tight turn before disappearing through the great arched gateway which, when the mansion was built, had admitted tall swaying carriages.

Still dizzy from the emotional impact of that one passionate kiss, Armorel turned and went slowly into the house. He had made her share his own feeling that a month was three weeks too long.

In the fortnight which followed, she was no longer puzzled by Sholto's avoidance of situations which strained his self-control. Instead, what troubled her more and more deeply as the day of their marriage drew nearer was her consciousness that, although he had succeeded in making her match his impatience for the consummation of their physical relationship, she had failed signally to make him utter one word of love for her.

She felt that her judgment was distorted by the strength with which he attracted her, and that perhaps, once he had made love to her, in his definition of the term, she would be released, as from a spell, and able to see life straight again.

She remembered Sholto telling Sidonie that the principal reason he intended to marry his protégée was because he thought she had courage, and hoped their children would inherit it. If indeed she did have the courage with which he credited her, thought Armorel, now was the time to bring it into play; to act boldly, and with resolution, not wavering uncertainly as she had done up to now, and not caring what anyone else thought, not even the man whose ring she wore, but acting upon her own most deep-seated beliefs. And the longer she thought on these lines, the stronger became her conviction that she could not go through with the marriage on its present basis although Sholto, and he alone, was the man with whom she wanted to experience love for the first time.

Fortunately, because of his detestation of publicity, they were having a very quiet civil wedding in a suburban *mairie* with only Adrian and Ellen as witnesses, followed by an informal lunch party before they flew to Athens to board *Isola* for a honeymoon among the Greek Islands. Even Jane would not be there, and indeed was not as yet privy to Armorel's engagement, being under the impression that her reason for lingering in Paris was to work there for a few weeks to see if she liked living there as much as in London.

So Armorel's secret decision not to go through with the marriage was not complicated by the social pressures of dozens of invitations to be cancelled, presents to be returned to their donors, elaborate catering arrangements to go to expensive waste. None of the usual ritual of a big, fashionable wedding was involved, and although her dress was by Jean-Louis Scherrer, the couturier favoured by the immensely elegant Madame Giscard d'Estaing and her good-looking daughter, Madame Philippe Guibout, it was a simple day dress for which she hoped, in time, to repay Sholto. She would never wear it, but she would keep it with her, a symbol of what might have been if only he had loved her as deeply as she loved him.

Three night before her wedding, after they had dined at a restaurant just outside Paris, Sholto brought her back and said goodnight to her in the courtyard because the Bocages were out, and he never came into the house late at night unless they were there.

When his car had gone, Armorel went up to her bedroom and left a note for Ellen on the dressing-table. This was a precaution against the unlikely event that Ellen might come to her room after their dinner party, and be alarmed at not finding her there. The note said only, 'Don't worry. Am with S. A.'

Armorel felt sure that Ellen would not be shocked, but would think it entirely natural for a couple so soon to be married to be lovers already. Armorel knew that her daughter Marie-France had shared a flat with her husband for some time before they were married.

Next she took from a cupboard the suitcase which she had packed earlier in the day. Being careful not to be seen by any of the servants, she left the house and walked a short distance until she was able to hail a taxi to take her to the Gare du Nord.

By the time she had left the suitcase at the *consigne*, and was in another taxi on the way to Sholto's flat, about forty minutes had passed since they had said goodnight. She was shivering with nerves when the taxi arrived at his address.

A night porter emerged from an office behind the desk which had to be passed by anyone using either the lifts or the staircase.

Not recognising her, because Sholto had never taken her there, he said, 'Yes, *mademoiselle*?'

She murmured Sholto's name and the number of his apartment. Perhaps she only imagined that the porter looked faintly surprised. It could be that, if the man had not had his job long, there had been no feminine visitors to No. 18 in his time.

One of the lifts was already at the ground floor, and the porter reached inside to press the button for the floor she wanted. He bade her a poker-faced goodnight. Clearly he did not expect her visit to be a brief one. At that hour of the night it was a reasonable conclusion that a girl going to a man's flat would be staying until morning.

Unless Sholto sends me away, she thought, as the lift passed above the first floor. But would any man send away a girl to whom, in forty-eight hours, he was expecting to be married?

The interval between her pressure on the bell and the door being opened was probably less than a minute, but it seemed more like five. Sholto was wearing the same black silk dressing-gown he had worn to come to her room at Gstaad on Christmas Eve.

At the sight of her, he raised an eyebrow. 'Hello, what brings you here?'

'May I come in?'

'Of course.' He moved aside for her to pass into the hall. An inner door leading into a lamp-lit sitting-room was open, and she walked through and dropped her bag on the nearest chair.

'Were you in bed?' she asked, beginning to unbutton the light cotton raincoat which she had put on over the silk shirt and velvet skirt in which she had dined with him.

'No, I was on the telephone until a few minutes before you rang. Is something wrong, Armorel?' As she shrugged off the coat he came to help her remove it. 'I thought you seemed slightly distraite earlier this evening. Eleventh-hour nerves?'

'Not really.' As he tossed the raincoat over the back of a sofa, she turned to him, moving close and placing her hands on his shoulders. 'As we were leaving the city tonight, we passed an accident. D'you remember? After you dropped me, I thought how cruelly ironic it would be if you were involved in a bad crash on your way back here, or if I should be knocked down tomorrow. Suddenly it seemed to be tempting Fate to put off being happy for forty-eight hours when we could be together now ... tonight. Let me stay with you, Sholto?'

As she spoke, she slid her arms round his neck and pressed herself invitingly against him. He put his hands on her hips, and for a long moment his shrewd eyes looked searchingly into hers and she knew an instant of panic in case he should read what lay at the back of her mind.

Then he bent his tall head and kissed her as he had done on the night of their engagement and only once since then; his mouth commanding her surrender, his hands slipping lower and spreading to seal her more closely against him, and to make her aware, as never before, of the strong driving force of his manhood which he could no longer keep leashed.

After a while he picked her up in his arms and carried her into another room where the curtains were open to let in a bright pool of moonlight. Shouldering the door shut behind him, he carried her to the side of a double bed which must already have had its cover removed because, later, she remembered seeing the paleness of the sheets and pillows in the half-darkness.

There, he set her on her feet, his hands searching for and finding the fastener at the back of her skirt and, when it had slipped to the floor, undoing the cuff and front buttons of her shirt. Underneath she was wearing only a sleek pure silk bra-slip and tights. Sholto sat on the side of the bed and drew her between his knees while his warm hands slipped under the lacy hem of the slip and roved slowly, caressingly upwards in search of the top of her tights. As he began to peel them off her, she stepped out of her high-heeled shoes and then, reaching her knees, he pulled her on to the bed beside him, and a few seconds later she was barefoot and next to naked.

The small clip between her shoulder-blades presented him with as little difficulty as her other fastenings, but she was only vaguely aware of her last scanty covering being taken from her because he was kissing her throat, and his hands were not only undressing her, but stroking and smoothing her quivering flesh while her own hands obeyed a responsive instinct to touch and explore his strong body; to plunge her fingers into his crisp dark hair and feel the shape of his head and the smooth skin cladding the muscles of his powerful shoulders.

She was suddenly, exultantly glad she had had no previous experience of the divinely sensuous reactions he was arousing. For she felt sure that neither Ben nor Kit, nor any of the men to whom she could have surrendered herself, would have known how to play with her body till she gasped and shuddered with rapture. With Sholto she felt no shyness; each caress prepared her for the next, made her ready and eager for each more intimate touch, more passionate kiss.

Yet, at the end, in the first moment of peace after storm, she found herself weeping, neither from pain nor disappointment—because it had been all she hoped for, and more—but because in the ultimate moments when they were as close to each other as two human beings could ever be, he had not said one word of love. He had brought her to a pitch of ecstasy which she would remember all her life; but never had he murmured her name, never made her feel she meant more to him than all the others with whom he had shared the same experience.

Hours later she woke to find herself lying in an attitude of total abandonment, and Sholto raised on one elbow, his hand slowly tracing a path from her throat to her thighs and, in between, lingering where her body was most sensitive.

She did not sleep again that night, but lay motionless but wakeful, staring at the unfamiliar shapes and shadows of his bedroom, wondering if she was a fool to want more than his name and position, his charm, and his skill as a lover—to want the one thing he withheld. His heart.

In the early hours of the morning, while he was still deeply asleep, she crept out of bed and, having gathered up her clothes, went into the other room to dress. She dared not risk using the bathroom, and when she looked in a mirror to comb her hair, there were marks round her eyes where his kisses and her tears had smudged the eye make-up she had not had the chance to remove. But what the night porter would think when she appeared in the lobby at five in the morning and asked him to call a cab for her, she did not care.

Her note of farewell and explanation she had written the day before, hoping against hope she might not have to leave it for him; hoping that, after he had made love to her, he might find himself saying, 'I love you.'

But that had not happened. She put the envelope in a prominent position in the sitting-room, and beside it she placed, in their boxes, her engagement ring, the cameo bracelet and the pearls.

Then, in great despair, she walked out of the flat, and out of his life.

CHAPTER SIX

She had found out in advance that there was a train which left Paris very early for the coast; but it was not until the Channel ferry drew away from the dockside that she felt she had made good her escape. Throughout the train journey she had been tense with the fear that Sholto might have woken up early and, guessing she meant to return to England, have driven like hell for leather in his fast car in order to intercept her while she was still on French soil.

She was in the saloon, holding a beaker of coffee between her ice-cold hands, when it struck her that, even now, she might not have got clean away. It was possible that although he had missed the ferry, he might have arrived in time to catch the first Hovercraft of the day which, taking about half an hour instead of one and a half hours, would get him to Dover before her.

However, one of the ship's officers was able to allay her fears on this score, although she felt that he looked at her with some curiosity, as if he suspected she was on the run from someone.

At Dover she caught a train to London and, there, a bus—to conserve her limited funds—to a cheap hotel which she knew of and where she meant to spend one night before going on to Bristol or Birmingham, or some large provincial city where she could get a job and re-think her life.

Having registered at the hotel, and been shown to her small, drab room, she locked herself in and collapsed on the bed in tears.

The night which followed was the most wretched of

her life, and in that she included all those nights in the Pacific when she had been frightened, cold, hungry and desperately thirsty, but still hopeful of being rescued. Now her life was not in danger, but she had no hope of ever being happy again, and what was the use of life without happiness?

To intensify her misery, she dreamt she was in Sholto's arms, and not only was he repeating the tender expertise with which, the night before, he had made her a woman, but this time he was telling her he loved her. It was one of those intensely vivid dreams from which she awoke as if from the deep, restful slumber after love, with a smile on her face and her body relaxed and ready to begin again.

Then the reality of it faded, and she found herself on her own in a narrow and sagging single bed, with no strong male body beside her to slake the passionate longings to which Sholto had introduced her, and which only he could satisfy. The thought that never again would she lie, sprawled in absolute surrender, while he worked his magic upon her pulsating flesh, was almost too terrible to bear. It was like having been illiterate, and then learnt to read, only to find oneself imprisoned for ever in a place without any books.

Bitterly, now, she regretted making him teach her what love was. Had she never experienced those transports, she would not have missed them as much as she knew she would in the future when, night after lonely night, sleep would elude her because, imprinted on her mind, was the indelible memory of all that had happened in the moonlit room the night before.

On what should have been her wedding day, Armorel was still in London, but planning to leave for Edinburgh the following morning. The idea of returning

to the country where her mother's family had their
origins had come to her suddenly, on the evening of her
second night in London, when too exhausted to summon
the energy for the next lap of her journey she had lain
all day on the bed in her dismal hotel room, in a kind
of torpor of unhappiness so disabling that she could
not be bothered even to go out to eat.

Part of this deep inertia had been caused by her
disinclination to set out on her lonely future in any
of England's major cities.

But when she had thought of Edinburgh, her spirits
had revived a little, and the following day she had forced
herself to eat a proper cooked breakfast, a light lunch
and substantial supper so that on the next day she
would be ready to move on.

She got as far as King's Cross. There, as she entered
the station, she saw on a newsvendor's board the headline BIG REWARD FOR MISSING BRIDE.

She bought a paper. The front page carried a photograph of Sholto, and of herself which she recognised as
having been taken by Chuck Bocage with his Christmas
present camera at Gstaad. The newspaper headline was
MILLIONAIRE OFFERS £25,000 REWARD FOR
NEWS OF RUNAWAY BRIDE.

Beneath this, she read, *Sholto Ransome, the publicity-
shy merchant prince, who never gives interviews to the
press and rarely is caught by the camera except at long
range, last night let down the barricade of privacy with
which he surrounds himself to announce that his secret
wedding to beautiful 21-year-old Armorel Baird, which
should have taken place in Paris today, has had to be
postponed because of his bride's disappearance. Mr
Ransome disclosed that Miss Baird had left a note for
him before leaving the house of Monsieur Adrian Bocage
and his wife, friends of Mr Ransome, with whom she*

had been staying. He would not reveal the text of the note beyond saying that his bride-to-be appeared to be suffering from pre-wedding nerves, and that as she was not staying with friends and had no relations to turn to, he was concerned for her well-being. Nor would he discuss the circumstances in which he and his fiancée met each other. He said they had known each other for two years and became engaged a month ago. Neither has been married before, but the good-looking millionaire, who is in his early thirties, is known to enjoy feminine company and his name has been linked with a number of beautiful women in the international jet set and film world. At one time it was thought that he and French actress, Sidonie Lamartine, might marry, but friends say their romance ended more than six months ago.

There was more, but Armorel had read enough to make her put down the paper with a muffled groan of dismay. The train for the north was not due to leave for half an hour. She sat down on a bench in the station concourse, and tried to think what to do.

Twenty-five thousand pounds was such an enormous amount of money that everyone who read the story would be on the alert to spot her. Even if, later today, she could dye her hair and change her appearance in other ways, she was more than likely to be recognised. Now, to start her new life would mean adopting another name, and how was she to overcome the difficulty of assuming an alias? Although the British did not, as yet, have identity cards, they did have taxation code numbers, National Insurance contribution cards, and medical files which were transferred when they moved.

To hide might be possible for a criminal, who had access to false papers, but not for herself, an honest person. Sholto had her cornered. There was no escape from the net which his wealth had spread for her.

Thus it was that when the train for Edinburgh left London Armorel was not on it, but in a taxi on her way to Avenfield House.

'Miss Baird!—oh, thank goodness! We've all been so worried about you,' exclaimed Mrs Benson, when she opened the door to her. 'Where have you been? What happened to you? Dear me, you don't look at all well. Did you have an attack of amnesia?'

'Not exactly,' said Armorel nervously, as the house-keeper drew her inside and took charge of the suitcase.

'I'm sure it would be no wonder, after all you went through in that terrible time in the Pacific,' said the housekeeper. 'Mrs Powers, your stewardess on the yacht, told me all about it when she was back in London recently. She stayed here, in the flat, when her husband was so dreadfully ill in hospital, you know. Mr Ransome was wonderfully kind to them. He always is, when any of his staff are in trouble. Now I'll make you a nice cup of tea, but first I must ring him, and put him out of his anxiety.'

'W-where is he?' Armorel asked her.

'He arrived in London yesterday morning. He felt you'd have come back to England. Excuse me, I shan't be five minutes.' She left Armorel in the sitting-room and hurried away to use the telephone in her own quarters.

When she came back, she announced, 'He'll be here in a quarter of an hour. Would you prefer tea or coffee?'

'Neither, thank you, Mrs Benson. I only had break-fast an hour ago. What did Mr Ransome say when you told him?'

'He was very relieved, the poor man. I've worked for him for five years, and I've never seen him as troubled as he was last night and this morning.'

'Yes, but what did he actually say to you?'

The housekeeper smiled. 'He said, "You keep her

there, Mrs Benson, or you'll find yourself out of a job".
But of course he was only joking. Do you know what I
think? I know it's too early in the day for anything
alcoholic, but I think one of my egg-nogs is what you
need to buck you up. You look very tired and pinched,
my dear.'

For the second time she disappeared, coming back
with a tall glass in which, she explained, was a mixture
of egg, sugar, milk and cognac poured over cracked
ice with a sprinkling of nutmeg on top.

Armorel had not finished drinking it when she heard
voices in the hall; Sholto's brusquely impatient, and
Mrs Benson's pacificatory. She set down the glass, her
hand trembling. She dreaded the coming confrontation.

When Sholto strode into the room, she could see at
once that he was ferociously angry with her.

'So you decided to come back!'—were his first furious
words, as he shrugged off the light-coloured raincoat he
was wearing over his other clothes and flung it aside on
a chair. 'What changed your mind, may one ask?'

At first, when she tried to reply, she found herself
tongue-tied with nervousness. Only by a great effort of
will did she finally manage to stammer, 'I—I couldn't
let you w-waste all that money—although I think it
was v-very unfair of you to use that kind of power
against me.'

'But you thought it quite fair to seduce me and then
to walk out on me?'

'You're being absurd,' she protested. 'How can a
girl seduce a man?'

'I don't know what else you would call it. You knew
damned well I had no intention of sleeping with you
until we were married, and wouldn't have done so if
you hadn't made it impossible for any man with blood
in his veins to resist you—particularly a man who

hadn't been to bed with a woman for over six months. If I'd deliberately aroused you to the point of allowing me to take you when I knew that was not what you wanted in your normal state of mind, I should have seduced you, should I not? Why is it different in reverse?'

'Well ... it just is, that's all,' she said, flushing. 'How was I to know you hadn't made love for six months? There was a time when it seemed to me you were practically always in bed with someone or other. Rosalind Plummer ... Sidonie ... that girl in New York.'

'What girl in New York?' he said blankly.

'How should I know who she was? I rang you up early one morning, and she answered the phone, and then you bit my head off. Probably, now, you can't even remember her name.' She saw by his expression that he could not. 'So it's rather ridiculous for you to accuse me of seducing you,' she went on. 'My—my intention was to give myself to you as ... as a kind of present, the only one I *could* give you—and also to make my own first experience of love something I should remember with pleasure and not disappointment.'

He came towards her and gripped her roughly by the shoulders. 'But with no intention of repeating it? You lay in my arms, knowing full well you meant to leave the next day?'

'Yes—but was that so wrong of me?'

'I should have said it was just about as irresponsible as it's possible to be,' he said savagely.

'Irresponsible? Why?'

'Did it ever cross your mind that there might be a price to pay for your night of pleasure? I should have thought you, of all people, wouldn't take the chance of history repeating itself.' Seeing her look of incomprehension, he put it more bluntly. 'You risked becoming pregnant.'

It was the first time such a thought had entered her mind. 'I—I don't think that's very likely.'

'I wonder how many human beings owe their existence to the same misguided confidence?' he said caustically. 'You may be ready to chance it, I'm not. No child of mine is going to be born without a legal father. Nor, I may add, am I prepared to finance a discreet operation.'

'I shouldn't expect you to. If—if I were pregnant, I should have to marry you,' she said reluctantly.

'But not otherwise?'

'No, I can't ... I can't.'

'Then it seems my only recourse is to make damn sure you are pregnant.'

Before she realised what he meant, he had scooped her up in his arms and was carrying her from the room and along the passage.

'Oh, please ... you can't! Put me down!' Even then she did not really believe that he meant to carry out the intention implicit in his words.

It was only when he halted outside a closed door and ordered her to open it that she began to wonder if he was capable of carrying out such a threat, or was merely trying to frighten her in revenge for—so he seemed to feel—making a fool of him.

'Open it!' he repeated.

Rather than make a fuss in a public part of the flat where Mrs Benson might come upon them, Armorel obeyed. The room within was, as she had expected, his bedroom; but even then she did not feel seriously alarmed, not even when he strode to the bed and dumped her upon it.

By the time he had returned to the door to close it and turn the key, she was on her feet on the far side of the wide bed.

He came slowly towards her, undoing his tie and collar

as he had in her room at the Bocage house, on the night of her twenty-first birthday party and again on the night of their engagement.

But this time he was not smiling. He looked both wrathful and ruthless and, for the first time, a tremor of fear stirred in her.

'Take off your clothes,' he commanded.

'I shall do no such thing,' she retorted, trying to keep her voice steady, but unable to stop herself backing nervously away from him.

Suddenly it seemed that the best thing to do was to make a dash for his bathroom and lock herself in until his hot temper had cooled.

She almost made it. But within a yard of the door a trap-like grasp snapped painfully hard on her wrist and he spun her into his arms and held her against him, imprisoned against his hard chest.

'Let me go! You can't do this,' she panted, her own temper rising.

'You don't know me very well yet. What I have, I hold,' he informed her. 'And you have given yourself to me. Did you really believe I should be satisfied with only one night with you? You may have enjoyed it. I hope you did. But from my point of view your embraces left a good deal to be desired. There is more to love than passive submission, and you still have everything to learn—starting now!'

For the second time within minutes he tossed her bodily on to the bed, and stood by the edge looking down at her while he unbuttoned his shirt and shrugged it off the broad shoulders which suddenly looked frighteningly powerful.

Paralysed with panic, she watched him unbuckle his belt and unzip his trousers. Keeping his eyes on her face, he took them off. His shoes were the slip-on type which did not have to be unlaced. He lifted his heels to remove them, letting them fall with dull thuds on the carpet behind him. Next he stripped off his socks. Then, still with that hot, implacable look in his eyes, he unfastened the strap of his wrist-watch and laid it aside on the night table, leaving only his pants to be removed.

Those gone, he rested one knee on the bed and reached for her.

She cringed away from him, trembling. 'You ... you won't enjoy raping me, Sholto.'

He gave a short bark of laughter. 'I shan't have to rape you, my girl. It's only a rape when the woman concerned is unwilling, and before we get to that stage you are going to be much more than willing.'

Although she knew it was futile, for pride's sake she had to fight him while he undressed her; struggling and squirming all the time he held her pinioned with one hand and took off her clothes with the other.

'If you don't keep still, your clothes will get torn,' he warned her, unfastening her blouse.

'I don't care! How can you *do* this? I thought you were a man, not an animal,' she flung at him.

'In the animal world the female never resists. She knows what is required of her, and submits to it,' he mocked her. 'There—that was your fault, my dear'— as the armhole stitching gave way because she had not remained still while he was sliding her sleeve down.

Then, with sudden impatience, he did not attempt to repeat the manoeuvre with the other sleeve, but took her collar in both hands and ripped the blouse down the back. He did the same with her bra, hooking his fingers inside the flimsy lace cups and exerting just enough pressure to make them part at the centre where a small bow of white satin ribbon had joined them together.

His warm palms took the place of the lace, moulding the swift agitated rise and fall of her bare flesh, and pressing her on to her back while she beat with clenched fists at his shoulders, hating herself for responding to the feel of his hands on her.

When he started to kiss her, at first she tried not to let his mouth fasten on hers and, when it did, not to let her lips soften and part. It was some hours since he had shaved, and his skin was rougher than it had been the night she went to his flat. His kisses were rougher as well. She began to realise how carefully he had held himself in check that night, making allowances for her innocence, gentling her into womanhood, never permitting his own experience to make him forget that for her it had been the first time.

Now he had no such compunction, and nor was there darkness to hide her shyness when he had finished undressing her, and was deliberately and expertly reducing her to the state of eager surrender which he had promised she would feel.

'Oh, no ... no ... oh, don't!' she gasped, as his devilishly expert hands caressed her to shuddering ecstasy.

Sometimes he would let her relax, kissing and touching her in ways which were soothing rather than inflaming; and sometimes he would ignore her, forcing her to a pitch of wanton abandonment which he watched with a kind of cruel amusement until, impelled by the longing to have the same effect on him, and stung by his slighting reference to her passive submission in Paris she reared up and flung herself at him, writhing and undulating against him, responding to instincts she had not known she possessed until, with a sudden groan, he locked her hard in his arms and rolled her backwards with an urgent strength which told her she had succeeded in driving him to the brink of the almost unbearable pleasure which, in an instant, would engulf them both.

When it was over, the all too brief implosion of indescribably lovely sensation which left her exhausted and content, she lay underneath him, gazing dreamily at the ceiling and wondering how many other people in London were entwined in the peaceful aftermath of love at this hour of the afternoon.

Then she must have dropped off to sleep for the next thing she knew was that she was alone, with only the lightness of a duvet covering her. She had been awake for a few minutes when the door opened and Sholto came in, fully dressed and carrying a tray which he placed on the night table.

'Mrs Benson has made a light lunch for you. I'm going out for a short time. I want your word that you won't attempt to leave this room until I come back. If you refuse to give it, I shall lock you in,' he said, in a matter-of-fact tone.

'I promise. Where are you going?'

He gave her a sardonic look. 'To arrange to make an honest woman of you first thing tomorrow. Where have you been staying? I'll pick up your baggage. You will want replacements for your blouse and bra. Not that you need to dress again today. Eat this'—with a nod at the tray—'and then have another nap. I want you refreshed when I come back. Ready for another lesson,' he added, his glance moving to her mouth. 'After six months' abstinence, I have considerable reserves of energy.'

One hand on the headboard, he swung down to plant a swift hard kiss on her lips, his free hand sliding under the duvet, passing possessively over the sleep-warm contours of her body.

Controlling an impulse to beg him to stay with her, Armorel told him she had already brought her suitcase to the flat. As he left the room, she was conscious of a burning impatience for his return, and was horrified at how easily she had fallen into total subjection to the power of his lips and his hands.

After a while she sat up and poured herself a cup of tea, and ate the crab and chicken sandwiches which Mrs Benson had cut for her.

Later, running her bath, she found her breasts and thighs had rosy marks on them; the light grazing made by his beard when he had rubbed his face against her softness. There were bruises too, on her arms where, at first, she had struggled and fought him.

But in general she felt more alive, more lazily voluptuous, more feminine than ever before in her life. She could not help pitying her aunt, and all other women like her, who had never felt the, to them, demeaning sensation of being in the power of a commanding male.

But this reaction was short-lived. It was not long before a revulsion of feeling set in, and she was once again oppressed by the carnal nature of their relationship. What else, really, had they in common?

She had climbed back into bed when someone tapped on the door and, concluding it must be Mrs Benson, Armorel covered her shoulders before she called, 'Come in.'

The clothes of which Sholto had stripped her had been tidied away out of sight, but even so it was possible that the housekeeper might suspect what had taken place in the bedroom a short time before. If she did, would she be shocked? She looked kind but rather strait-laced; not the sort of person who would have allowed her husband to anticipate their marriage vows or, even afterwards, cast off all restraints as Armorel knew that she herself had during her love battle with Sholto. Yet how could anyone tell what banked fires of passionate feeling other people concealed from the world? At heart the sedate Mrs Benson might be a houri, she thought with a stifled laugh as the housekeeper entered.

'Madame Lamartine is on the telephone, Miss Baird. She wanted to speak to Mr Ransome, but I explained that he was out at present. Will you have a word with her? I did say you might be asleep and, if so, I wouldn't disturb you.'

'I'll speak to her. Thank you, Mrs Benson.'

Armorel waited until the other woman had withdrawn before she reached a bare arm towards the bedside telephone.

'Sidonie? It's me—Armorel.'

'I've just heard from Ellen Bocage that you have come out of hiding. I couldn't resist ringing up to find out if you were all right. I am still very fond of Sholto, you know, and of you, too, *chérie*.' It was a good line. The actress's voice was as clear as if she were speaking from another flat in the same block.

'I'm fine, thank you. Sidonie.'

'Why is Sholto not there with you? What has happened between you two now? I don't understand why you ran away in the first place. You may tell me it's not my business, if you wish, but one can't help being very curious when a girl backs out of a marriage which is what most women dream of.'

'Do you remember my twenty-first birthday party?'

'Of course.'

'During the evening you and Sholto went for a stroll in the garden, and he told you he was going to marry me. Accidentally, I overheard that conversation. When you asked if he was in love with me, he said he wasn't. He had other reasons for wanting me to be his wife. I ran away because I *am* in love with him, and I felt I couldn't bear to go through with it when he didn't love me.'

'You mean he has never told you he loves you? But how extraordinary!'

'Why extraordinary? On his side, it isn't a love match. It's more like one of those marriages which used to be arranged by people's parents.'

'But that is nonsense!' Sidonie exclaimed. 'I don't know why he has never told you he loves you, but he does—you may be sure of that. Ellen Bocage told me he was frantic with anxiety. It shows how desperate he was that he told the story to the press. The reward, I know, means little to him, but his privacy is of the greatest importance. He detests the limelight. Love is not a matter of words but of actions, *ma chérie*. If he treats you with love, does it matter if he does not say what is in his heart?'

'I suppose not—if the feeling is there. Anyway, we're going to be married after all. That's why he's out now—to arrange it.'

'So you aren't returning to Paris?'

'Apparently not.'

'No doubt, now that you are back with him, he wants to avoid further publicity. Only *les Bocage* and I know he is in London, not Paris.' Sidonie gave a low chuckle. 'I can imagine he was not in a very loving mood when you reappeared. Like the parents of a lost child, he would react with anger rather than affection. I should not be surprised to hear he had spanked you very hard for giving him such a bad time.'

'No, he didn't spank me, but he was rather angry at first,' said Armorel, thinking, 'And that's a masterly understatement!'

'I'm sure he was,' said the actress. 'And that also shows that he cares for you very much. Had I, or any other of

the women of his bachelor life, ever disappeared, he
would not have been troubled. He would merely have
shrugged and looked round for someone else to amuse
him. But with you he is serious, I'm sure of it.'

'Are you?'

The Frenchwoman must have heard the lingering
doubt in Armorel's tone. She said, 'Yes, but if he were
not, what is important is that he wants to marry you, and
a wife can always make her husband love her, if she
puts her mind to it. She is at the centre of his life. If she
takes pains to make herself desirable, and if she considers his comfort down to the last, smallest detail, how
can she fail?'

'I suppose not,' Armorel agreed.

They talked for a few minutes longer, and then
Sidonie rang off, leaving Armorel to ponder her advice.

*A wife can always make her husband love her, if she
puts her mind to it.* Was it true?

She could see how it might well be true in the case of
the man in the street. A wife who was a splendid cook,
and an economical and efficient housekeeper, could make
all the difference to an ordinary man's comfort. But
Sholto had a team of people to provide him with
superb food, to valet his clothes, and to ensure that
wherever he was living was always in immaculate order.
Children, and perhaps companionship, were what he
required of a wife.

He came back to find her curled in a chair by the
window, wearing a gaily-coloured happi coat which she
had found in his wardrobe and which he must have been
given on a flight to Japan.

'Mrs Benson has gone out for a couple of hours, and
she must have put my suitcase in one of your visitors'
rooms. So, having promised not to leave this room, I
borrowed this,' she explained.

She smiled as she said it; her mind now firmly made up. She had done with all her further soul-searching. She was his for ever, heart and mind, but she would not continue to yearn for more than he was able to give her. The past few days had made her realise the truth of the saw that half a loaf was better than no bread.

He said, 'It's all arranged. We'll be married at ten o'clock tomorrow, and fly to Athens as we should be doing at this moment. The only thing I haven't fixed is the witnesses. Would you like to ask your friend Jane Bruce to be one of them?'

'Yes, very much.'

'You'd better ring her up now. Invite her to come here for dinner if she has no other engagement.'

She got up and padded barefoot across the thick soft blue carpet, not in the direction of the telephone but towards him.

'Sholto, have you begun to forgive me for worrying you, and for having to talk to the press because of me?'

There was none of the earlier fierceness in his face as he looked down at her, only his usual quizzical half-smile.

'You're going to have first-hand experience of why I cherish my privacy. When you've run the gauntlet of the photographers who are encamped in the main hall downstairs waiting to get a picture of you, you'll understand why I try to keep out of the papers,' he answered.

'How do they know I've come back to you?'

'I thought it best to announce it, to save Miss Pike and other people on my staff from dealing with any more calls from members of the public who think they've seen you. The London evening papers will probably Stop Press it, and I fear that what was to have been our "secret wedding" will now take place in a glare of publicity,' he said sardonically.

*

Forty-eight hours later Armorel found herself back on board the gleaming white yacht on which her relationship with the man who was now her husband had begun. They were anchored off one of the more remote bays of an Aegean island where the largest fishing port had a tourist trade which justified the daily delivery of various foreign newspapers one day out of date. This was how she came to be lying in the sun on the afterdeck, with a large straw hat shading her eyes and a copy of a well-known daily newspaper in her hands.

It was a paper which Sholto disliked for its sensationalism, and it had not been brought on board at his orders. A member of the galley crew, sent to town to buy freshly caught fish, had brought it back with him. Mrs Powers had seen it and thought that, whatever her employer's opinion might be, his bride would be interested in a picture of herself emerging from the register office where she had changed her name from Baird to Ransome.

Armorel was interested. As she studied the photograph, which covered half the front page, she thought that, in spite of the difficulties immediately preceding the wedding, they looked a very happy couple. She was smiling at Sholto, and he at her, in a way which must convince the paper's readers that it was a love match. Although now she came to consider it, she had often seen similar pictures of couples in the public eye who, only a year or two after exchanging equally bright bridal smiles, were reported to be splitting up.

A paragraph at the foot of the page caught her eye. *Ex-girl-friend reveals tycoon's love at first sight for bride whose life he saved. Exclusive full story inside.*

Hastily opening the paper at the centre pages, she found a photograph of Rosalind Plummer, no longer blonde and described in the caption as 'The vivacious redhead who was part of the reformed millionaire's colourful past.'

She had just finished reading the text alongside the picture when a hand fell lightly on her shoulder, making her give a violent start.

'Oh ... I didn't hear you coming back,' she exclaimed, looking up at Sholto who she had thought would be occupied in his study for at least an hour.

'Where did you get hold of that rag?' he asked, sitting down on the lounger alongside hers, and indicating the newspaper.

'Mrs Powers thought I should like to see the picture of us on the front page. Would it be possible to get a copy of it?'

'I should think so, if you want one. May I see?'

Reluctantly she handed the paper to him, hoping he wouldn't notice the reference to the story she had been reading when he startled her. But she might have known that his keen eyes wouldn't miss anything, and when he turned to the centre pages and began reading Rosalind's revelations, she expected at every moment to see his dark eyebrows contract and the lines of his mouth begin to harden with anger. But although one eyebrow rose higher as he scanned the highly-coloured account of how Armorel had come into his life, it did not appear to enrage him.

'I wonder how much they paid her for that taradiddle,' was his dry comment, as he closed the tabloid and tossed it on to the foot of Armorel's lounger.

Relieved that he wasn't furious, she ventured to say, 'It makes me sound like the Lady of Shalott, floating peacefully along, looking beautiful, instead of the wreck that I was, whom nobody, least of all you, could possibly love at first sight.'

'No, you weren't at your best the first time I saw you,'

he agreed. Then, to her much greater surprise than when he had come upon her a few minutes earlier, he added, 'I don't think one's deepest affections, whether for friends or one's wife, ever come into being overnight. I suppose I became aware that you had a power over me much stronger than any other woman's one night in your room at Gstaad.'

'A power over you?' she echoed.

Her legs were stretched out in front of her, but he had his feet on the deck, and he moved from his lounger to hers and took hold of her hands.

'Love is what it's generally known as, but that's not a word I've ever found easy to use ... or a state which I wanted to be in. I didn't realise that I was until the day you disappeared.'

'You love me?' she asked, in a hushed voice. 'You've never said so. Not even when——' She left the sentence unfinished.

'Not even in bed with you. No, I know,' he agreed. 'It's taken me a few days to get used to the idea, and to be able to admit that I couldn't now, live without you.'

'Oh, Sholto!' Her voice was unsteady, her eyes bright with quick tears of joy.

He took her into his arms and, holding her close to him, said, 'You reacted like this to Jane's Christmas stocking. You'd never had one before, and suddenly I wanted to give you everything you'd never had in life. Instead of which you gave me the one thing I'd never had from a woman—a present from which you'd had to sacrifice something of great value to you. I should have known then, shouldn't I, that you would never take me for a ride?'

'*Have* you ever been taken for a ride? Is that why you once spoke of love in such a contemptuous way to me?' she asked, leaning back in his arms to look up at his face.

'No, I haven't. But I've always been very much aware that, with the exception of Sidonie, all the women I've known have cared as little for me as I for them.'

'Could you have loved Sidonie, if she hadn't been wedded to her career?'

'No, I could never have loved anyone but you. You're all I want in a woman—intelligent, kind, funny, loving, and, in my eyes, incomparably beautiful. God knows why it took me so long to face the fact that I'm insanely in love with you as any young boy.'

'But it *is* very hard to accept that one's whole life hinges on someone else. I know. I fought against loving you.'

They became aware of a sound disturbing the hot golden peace of the afternoon.

Looking up at the vivid blue sky, Sholto said, 'I thought it wouldn't be long before someone reported that *Isola* was in the Aegean, and the press came looking for us. That helicopter coming towards us was probably hired by a photographer. Let's be kind to him, shall we?'

As the helicopter came near the yacht and hovered beside her, they stood by the stern rails, smiling and waving for the cameraman focussing on them from his seat by the aircraft's pilot.

Then Sholto's arm tightened round Armorel's waist, and he said, 'Now, let's go below.'

And, looking up, she saw at last her own deep love for him reflected in the smiling grey eyes of her husband.

Mills & Boon Classics

The very best of Mills & Boon
romances, brought back for those of
you who missed reading them
when they were first published.

in
February
we bring back the following four
great romantic titles.

THE CASTLE IN THE TREES
by Rachel Lindsay

The very name of the Castle in the Trees fascinated Stephanie,
and the reality was even more intriguing than she had imagined.
But there was mystery there too. Why did Miguel and Carlos
de Maroc hate each other? Stephanie found out at last, but
only at the cost of losing her heart.

ISLAND OF PEARLS
by Margaret Rome

Many English girls go to Majorca for their holiday in the secret
hope of meeting romance. Hazel Brown went there and found
a husband. But she was not as romantically lucky as she
appeared to be — for Hazel's was a husband with a difference . . .

THE SHROUDED WEB
by Anne Mather

For several very good reasons Justina wished to keep the news
of her husband's death from her frail, elderly aunt. Then she
heard of the Englishman Dominic Hallam, who was in hospital
suffering from amnesia, and the germ of an idea came into
her mind . . .

DEVIL IN A SILVER ROOM
by Violet Winspear

Margo Jones had once loved Michel, so when he died she found
herself going to look after his small son in the French chateau
of Satancourt. There Margo met Paul Cassilis, Michel's
inscrutable brother, to whom women were just playthings,
but in "Miss Jones" was to find one woman who was determined
not to be.

Doctor Nurse Romances

and February's
stories of romantic relationships behind the scenes
of modern medical life are:

NURSE ON WARD NINE
by Lisa Cooper

It was a wrench for Claire Melville to leave home —
and Martin — to nurse at the Princess Beatrice
Hospital, and on Ward Nine she encountered hazards
she had never expected — not least that cold-eyed,
moody Doctor Andrew MacFarlane!

SATURDAY'S CHILD
by Betty Neels

Saturday's child works hard for a living . . . . And so
did Nurse Abigail Trent, plain and impoverished and
without hope of finding a husband. Why did she have
to fall in love with Professor Dominic van Wijkelen,
who hated all women and Abigail in particular?

Order your copies today from your local paperback retailer.

Choose from this selection of

Mills & Boon

Golden Treasury

COLLECTION